WELCOME TO A KEEPSAKE TREASURY of timeless stories about Kirsten Larson, a pioneer girl growing up in the wilderness on the edge of America's western frontier. Kirsten leaves all she's ever known to come to the New World, a place where people don't speak her language or wear clothes like hers or know about the traditions she holds dear. Fitting in and feeling at home takes time, but because girls like Kirsten worked so hard and never lost heart, America became a home for people from all over the world who wanted a better life and needed a fresh start.

Together for the first time, these classic stories have captured girls' imaginations for more than a decade. Step inside Kirsten's world of wilderness and prairie, new friends and new beginnings, and be inspired all over again.

# KIRSTEN'S
## *Story*
## *Collection*

BY JANET SHAW

ILLUSTRATIONS BY
RENÉE GRAEF

American Girl.

Published by Pleasant Company Publications
Copyright © 2001 by Pleasant Company
All rights reserved. No part of this book may be used or reproduced
in any manner whatsoever without written permission except in the
case of brief quotations embodied in critical articles and reviews.
For information, address: Book Editor,
Pleasant Company Publications,
8400 Fairway Place, P.O. Box 620998,
Middleton, WI 53562.

Manufactured in China.
01 02 03 04 05 06 07 08 LEO 12 11 10 9 8 7 6 5 4 3 2 1

PICTURE CREDITS
The following individuals and organizations have generously given permission to
reprint images contained in "Looking Back": pp. 360–361— *Saint Paul, Minnesota,
1855* by S. Holmes Andrews (detail), Minnesota Historical Society; Early Settler Life
Series, Crabtree Publishing Company, New York; *Across the Continent: Westward the
Course of Empire Takes Its Way,* Currier and Ives, courtesy of George A. Poole III
Collection, The Newberry Library, Chicago; pp. 362–363—State Historical Society
of Wisconsin CF 54844; State Historical Society of Wisconsin WHi(H44)94; photo
courtesy State Historical Society of Iowa, Frank E. Foster Collection; pp. 364–365—
State Historical Society of Wisconsin WHi(X3)19930; © Bettmann/CORBIS; *He That
Tilleth the Land Shall Be Satisfied,* Philadelphia Museum of Art: The Collection of
Edgar William and Bernice Chrysler Garbisch, photo by Graydon Wood, 1990.

Cover Backgrounds by Jean-Paul Tibbles and Mike Wimmer
Vignette Illustrations by Paul Lackner and Keith Skeen

**Library of Congress Cataloging-in-Publication Data**

Shaw, Janet Beeler, 1937–
Kirsten's story collection / by Janet Shaw ; illustrations, Renée Graef ;
vignettes, Paul Lackner, Keith Skeen.

p. cm.—(The American girls collection)

Contents: Meet Kirsten—Kirsten learns a lesson—Kirsten's surprise—
Happy birthday, Kirsten!—Kirsten saves the day—Changes for Kirsten.
ISBN 1-58485-443-X
1. Children's stories, American. [1. Swedish Americans—Fiction.
2. Frontier and pioneer life—Minnesota—Fiction. 3. Minnesota—Fiction.]
I. Graef, Renée, ill. II. Lackner, Paul, ill. III. Skeen, Keith, ill. IV. Title. V. Series.
PZ7.S53423 Kiu 2001
[Fic]—dc21   2001021782

# TABLE OF CONTENTS

### KIRSTEN'S FAMILY AND FRIENDS

# KIRSTEN'S FAMILY

**PAPA**
*Kirsten's father, who
is sometimes gruff
but always loving.*

**MAMA**
*Kirsten's mother, who
never loses heart.*

**KIRSTEN**
*A nine-year-old
girl who moves with
her family to a new home
on America's frontier
in 1854.*

**LARS**
*Kirsten's fourteen-year-
old brother, who is
almost a man.*

**PETER**
*Kirsten's mischievous
brother, who is
five years old.*

**BRITTA**
*Kirsten's baby
sister, who's born
sooner than expected!*

**ANNA**
*Kirsten's seven-
year-old cousin.*

**LISBETH**
*Kirsten's eleven-
year-old cousin.*

**UNCLE OLAV**
*Kirsten's uncle, who
came to America six
years before Kirsten
and her family.*

**AUNT INGER**
*Kirsten's aunt, who
helps the Larsons feel
at home in America.*

# KIRSTEN'S FRIENDS

MARTA
*Kirsten's best friend
on the long trip
from Sweden
to Minnesota.*

SINGING BIRD
*Kirsten's secret Indian
friend, who calls her
"Yellow Hair."*

MISS WINSTON
*Kirsten's teacher,
who helps her
learn English.*

FOR MY MOTHER,
NADINA FOWLER

# 1854
# MEET
# KIRSTEN

## *An American Girl*

# AMERICA!

"That's America!" Kirsten said happily. She stood at the ship's railing with her friend Marta and pointed to the green strip of land beyond the waves. Over-head, the tall sails creaked in the wind.

Marta shaded her eyes and pressed against the railing as though that would make the *Eagle* sail faster. "I can't wait to walk on land again," she said, and shivered.

Kirsten touched her friend's thin arm. "Are you cold?" she asked. "Let's go sit where the wind isn't so strong." She tucked her rag doll, Sari, into her shawl and walked to a coil of rope that was as high as a barrel. Then she hitched up her skirt and

1

climbed into a space just big enough for two girls to sit knee to knee and forehead to forehead. Marta crawled in after her.

It was warmer here in the coiled rope, but the wind still whistled overhead. Kirsten took her handkerchief from her pocket and made a cape for Sari. Marta's doll wore her apron like a shawl. "Soon we'll be on land again," Marta told her doll. "Don't worry about the wind."

Kirsten pulled a piece of hard, dry bread from her apron pocket and broke it in two. She and Marta fed their dolls before they chewed the bread themselves. "What's the very first thing you want to do in America?" Kirsten asked.

"I want to pick an apple," Marta said dreamily. "There are apples everywhere in America."

"Apples!" When Kirsten said the word she could almost taste the crisp, delicious fruit. "We'll pick cherries, too!" she said.

"And we'll get fresh bread," Marta added. "I think we'll be there by tonight, don't you?"

"Not if it storms again," Kirsten answered. She peered up at the darkening clouds and pulled her shawl more closely around her shoulders. Above

2

her head she saw the sailors crawling into the
rigging to adjust the sails. Then she heard Papa's
voice.

"Kirsten, where are you?" he called.

Kirsten stood and shouted, "Here I am, Papa!"
Strands of blond hair pulled loose from her braids
and whipped across her cheeks when she raised her
head above the ropes.

Papa's black wool jacket flapped like a gull's
wings as he crossed the deck. "There's a storm
coming," Papa said. "It could be dangerous. The
coast is rocky here, and the wind is getting stronger."

Papa lifted Kirsten out of the coiled rope. Then he pulled Marta out, too. "Come below where we'll be safe," he said.

The clouds rolled like water boiling in Mama's black iron pot. The tops of the waves turned white and crashed over the sides of the ship. They dashed onto Kirsten's boots as she scrambled toward the opening into the hold. "Hurry!" Papa said. He held tightly to Kirsten's and Marta's hands.

As Kirsten climbed down the ladder into the hold, her spirits sank. Of course she didn't want to be washed overboard by the waves, but it was awful to stay in this small room below the deck. For more than two months, twenty Swedish families had been cramped together here. Each family shared one or two of the bunks that lined the walls, and everything they owned was stored in large trunks which stood at the ends of the bunks. The air smelled sour now, and it would be worse when people got seasick. No fresh air could come in when the sailors locked the trap-door against the waves. And the hold was dark, even in the middle of the afternoon. Just one oil lantern swung and sputtered over some tables in the middle of the room. Kirsten could barely see Mama, who was lying on her side in the narrow bunk she shared with Kirsten.

"Here you are," Mama said as Kirsten crawled up beside her. "I asked Papa to find you. I don't know where you can hide on such a small ship."

"Marta and I were playing. We could see land before the storm blew up," Kirsten said.

Mama sighed. "I prayed there would be no more storms so I could be strong when we land in America," she said. She had been sick since the first day they came aboard the ship, and storms made her feel worse.

"You'll be strong soon, I'm sure of it. Don't lose heart, Mama," said Kirsten. But now the wind howled like a pack of wolves. The waves beat against the ship's hull, next to Kirsten's head, and the ship tossed as though it might tip over.

Outside there was a loud crash. Mama put her arm over Kirsten's shoulder. "Don't fall off the bunk," she warned. Buckets tumbled over one another, and old Mr. Peterson's trunk skidded across

5

*The waves beat against the ship's hull, next to Kirsten's head,
and the ship tossed as though it might tip over.*

the wet floor. The lantern swung wildly, then dropped beneath a table.

"Mama, Lars says the coast is full of rocks. Do you think we'll be blown onto them?" Kirsten asked. She could barely hear her own words above the roar of the storm.

"Don't think about the rocks," Mama said. "Let's think about Uncle Olav's letter instead. Do you remember your Uncle Olav?"

Kirsten had heard about Uncle Olav so many times she *thought* she remembered him. "Tell me," she said. She snuggled close to Mama and tried not to think about the howling storm.

"Olav left Sweden six years ago, when you were just three," Mama said. "He thought he could make a better life in America. And last year, he wrote to tell us about his new farm. The land is rich and good there, and he needs our help."

"In Minne-sota," Kirsten said, stumbling over the strange word.

"Yes, in Minnesota," Mama answered. "Now you tell me something."

"Uncle Olav married Aunt Inger in America," Kirsten said. She thought this was the best part of the story. "Aunt Inger came from Sweden, too."

"That's right," said Mama. "Olav said he married a widow with two daughters."

"My cousins, Anna and Lisbeth," Kirsten finished. "We'll be friends, don't you think?"

"Of course," said Mama. "We'll live on the same farm, and they'll be right next door."

The waves still pounded against the ship. In the dark hold, Kirsten hugged Sari's rag body and whispered, "We're almost there. We're almost home." She tried to imagine a farm right next door to her new cousins. She hoped this American home would be just like the one she left in Sweden, with the maple tree by the door.

When the storm finally passed, Kirsten felt like the barn cat she'd once fished out of the well. Her skirt and shawl were wet and stained. Her boots were soaked. But everyone was safe, the sky was clear, and the *Eagle* was sailing toward the green coast once more. Kirsten watched the seagulls swoop and dive as she stood on the deck with Mama and Papa.

"I smell the earth again," Papa's voice boomed. He held Peter, who was five, on his hip.

Mama smiled at the shore as though she greeted a friend. She leaned toward Papa, and Kirsten heard her whisper, "So many times I lost hope that we'd all make it to America."

"You're a brave woman," Papa answered. "You have heart. I'm proud of you and our children."

Kirsten's brother Lars, who was always talking with the sailors, pushed through the crowd just then. "The sailors say we'll land in New York tomorrow morning," Lars said.

"That's wonderful!" Mama replied. "We'll have fresh bread for breakfast, and I'll find a place to wash our clothes."

"They say we can't leave the ship until the health inspector lets us," Lars added.

"What's the health inspector?" Kirsten asked.

"He's a doctor who will look at everyone on the ship. No one who is sick can stay in America," Lars explained.

"But Mama's sick!" Peter cried. He held out his arms, and Mama hugged him.

"Mama has only been seasick," Papa said in his deep voice. "Almost everyone gets seasick on the ocean. The health inspector looks for illnesses like typhoid and cholera. Illnesses that kill people."

"No one on our ship has cholera," Lars said.

"That's right," Papa replied. "You see, Peter, we don't need to worry. Let's see you smile again. Tomorrow we'll be in New York, and then we'll start our journey to Minnesota."

When the *Eagle* finally docked in New York harbor and the health inspector said that they could leave the ship, Lars bounded down the gangplank. Peter scrambled right behind him. Mama and Papa went next, then Kirsten. She held Sari tightly.

Kirsten was bursting to run and turn circles on the grass she saw near the docks. She was surprised when she stepped off the gangplank and the ground seemed to spin around her. In Sweden, it had been steady under her feet. Here in America, it swayed and rolled like the ship she'd just left. She grabbed Papa's hand. "Why am I so dizzy?" she asked.

"We're all used to the rocking of the ship," Papa answered. "Now we have to get used to dry land all over again."

For a minute, Kirsten stood still. Then she turned and looked back at the *Eagle*. When they boarded the small ship, no one had known what to expect. There had been dangerous storms at sea. They had been sick. But at last they had arrived in America.

*What will happen now?* Kirsten wondered. But she was more curious than afraid. On wobbly legs, she followed Mama and Papa up the path into the park near the dock.

# LOST

Kirsten sat under an oak tree with
Mama and Peter. She patted down the
grass to make a bed for Sari. Although
it was only June, the grass here in the
park was already as dry as straw. Summer was so
hot in America! Three months ago, when they left
the farm in Sweden, Kirsten had needed her wool
skirt and shawl. Now her clothes were much too
heavy. Even without her quilted petticoats she
was hot.

Peter lay on his stomach, watching the road.
He was on the lookout for Papa and Lars, who had
gone to buy tickets for the rest of their journey. Papa
promised that later he would take Peter and Kirsten

to buy bread and milk. Kirsten couldn't wait. She wanted to explore this new town, New York. But Mama wouldn't let her go by herself. Swedish children could easily get lost here in America, Mama warned.

While Papa was gone, Kirsten watched the New Yorkers stroll by. The women and girls wore flowered dresses with lots of ruffles. The men wore tight trousers and white jackets. Kirsten looked down at her own tattered clothes. The only fine thing she wore was the amber heart her grandmother had given her on the day they said good-bye. "Oh, Mama, I wish we could wear such pretty dresses," Kirsten said. "Only the people from the ships look like this."

"Our clothes are dry and clean. We don't need to be ashamed," Mama answered. Her cheeks were pink again, and now she smiled. "Besides, how could I milk a cow if I wore so many ruffles?"

Peter made a face. He hated to dress up, even for church. Then his frown turned into a grin and he jumped to his feet. "Here come Papa and Lars!" he called.

13

Lars held a handful of cherries. Papa scooped more fruit from the knapsack slung over his arm. He gave one big handful to Peter and another to Kirsten. Then he knelt beside Mama to share what was left.

"I've never seen such huge black cherries," Mama said.

"Everything in America is big!" Lars announced. "Wait until you see New York."

"And there will be more to see tomorow," Papa added in a hearty voice. "I just bought our tickets for the trip west. We leave in the morning."

"Did you find an honest agent?" Mama asked with a worried frown. "Old Mr. Peterson was cheated of his money by a dishonest agent. I didn't know there were so many thieves in America."

Papa put his hand on her shoulder. "Yes, our agent is a good man. He left Sweden four years ago, and he knows English well. And he helped me change our money at a bank."

Mama still sighed. "It's such a long way to Minnesota," she said.

"But the agent will guide us all the way to the Mississippi River. He says we'll have to travel only a few weeks more," Papa replied. "And now that we're on land, we'll get our strength back quickly." He smiled. "Don't lose heart."

Mama smiled back. "No, I won't lose heart now."

Peter tugged the sleeve of Papa's shirt. "Let's go buy our milk and bread!" he said.

Mama handed Kirsten the milk pitcher. "Stay close to your father," she warned Kirsten and Peter. "Remember, you don't speak English yet."

Papa took Peter's hand as they walked along the wide, crowded street called Broadway. Kirsten skipped beside them. She held the milk pitcher tightly in one arm and Sari in the other.

Kirsten had never seen so many horses, so many wagons, buggies, carts. Men and women filled the sidewalks. Children darted among them. In her small town in Sweden, Kirsten had known everyone she met. Here, everyone was a stranger. These Americans chattered, called, and shouted all around her. Kirsten couldn't understand a single word they said.

She walked with Papa past carts full of onions

and potatoes. Chickens and ducks
fluttered and squawked in their
coops as they waited to be sold.
"Papa," Kirsten begged, "slow
down! I want to look around."

Now there were candy stores, shops that sold
tobacco, candles, tinware, cloth—oh, everything.
"Here's the bread shop," Papa said. Round loaves of
wheat bread were stacked inside the shop window.
Papa carefully counted out two American coins, and
the shopkeeper gave him several rolls. He handed
one to Kirsten and one to Peter. "Now we'll get
milk," he said.

The fresh bread was soft and sweet. Kirsten
tried to eat slowly to make it last. She kept her
eye on Papa's broad shoulders as she walked
down the busy street, munching. She saw women
holding huge baskets heaped with fruit. She
couldn't understand what the women said, but
the red berries in their baskets reminded her of
the delicious cloudberries her grandmother gathered
in Sweden.

Kirsten paused a moment by a gray-headed
berry seller. Then a boy carrying a tray of silvery

fish bumped her. She almost stumbled over a small black boy who polished a man's boots. "Wait, Papa!" she called over the racket of the horses' hooves on cobblestones.

But Papa was gone. Kirsten had lost sight of him in the crowd.

Clutching Sari, Kirsten ran. She squeezed between women with their shopping baskets. "Papa, wait for me!" she called. But she didn't see Papa. Lots of little boys chased through the crowd, but not one of them was Peter.

*Maybe Papa and Peter are already at the milk shop,* Kirsten thought. *Maybe they're waiting for me to come with the milk pitcher.* She hurried along, looking in each shop window for cheese and barrels of milk.

Where was the milk shop? Was it on the other side of the street? Kirsten climbed around pigs that poked their snouts in the trash of the gutter. Then she dodged in front of a buggy, ran across the street, and headed down the row of shops. She couldn't find the milk shop anywhere. And this side of the street was even more crowded with shoppers. The babble of their voices made her head swim. "Papa!" Kirsten called. Her cry was lost in the noisy street.

*"Papa!" Kirsten called.*
*Her cry was lost in the noisy street.*

Kirsten tucked her necklace into her collar and hugged the milk pitcher tightly. Mama had said there were thieves in New York, a lot of thieves. They would steal anything. "Papa! Papa!" Kirsten shouted. Papa was nowhere to be found.

*Maybe I should go back to the park,* Kirsten said to herself. *Mama's waiting there.* But now Kirsten realized she didn't know where the park was, either. Which way had she come with Papa? How many corners had they turned?

She asked a woman with a baby in her arms, "Please, where is the park by the river?" The woman kept walking as though she hadn't even heard Kirsten.

"The park?" Kirsten asked a tall boy with black hair. He said something to his friend, and they laughed at her.

"Help me!" Kirsten cried out. "Please help me!" No one even glanced at her. Couldn't anyone in this big crowd understand that she was lost?

Sun reflected off the cobblestones, and the smell of garbage made Kirsten dizzy. Her head spun as though she were seasick on the ship. But this time she wasn't seasick. She was frightened. What if she couldn't find Papa? What if she couldn't find the park and Mama? What would happen to her in this huge city if she couldn't find her family?

Again, she began to run. She stumbled and bumped into barrels. When a dog nipped at her ankles, she didn't stop running. Now she was on a different part of the street, where rough-looking men in bloody aprons sold wild game and meat. Gutted rabbits, squirrels, and deer hung from poles. Sides of pork dangled from sharp hooks. The buzz of flies hummed in her ears.

She headed back the other way, but she seemed to have turned onto a different street. The houses were all crowded together, and there were no shops at all. Papa would never look for her here! And every turn she took might lead her farther away from the park where Mama waited.

Kirsten wanted to be brave. She wanted to have heart, like Mama. But she sank down on the steps of a brown house, hid her face in her doll's skirt, and wept. Tears ran between her fingers and dropped onto her lap. "Oh, Sari," she cried, "what if we can't find Mama and Papa? Will they go to Minnesota without us?"

After what seemed like a long time, Kirsten felt a touch on her shoulder. A brown-haired young woman in a long blue apron stood beside her. When the woman spoke, her voice was gentle. She seemed to want to know what was wrong.

"I'm lost!" Kirsten said. The woman didn't understand. She looked puzzled and shook her head, and more tears ran down Kirsten's cheeks.

The woman spoke again. Now she made a motion as if she were pouring. Did she want the milk pitcher? Kirsten clutched it to her chest, and the woman went back inside the house.

"Sari, what will we do!" Kirsten sobbed.

Then the woman was back. This time she held out a tin cup of water. Gratefully, Kirsten drank until there wasn't a drop left. "*Tack!*" she said.

The woman smiled and sat down on the step. She understood "thank you." But how could Kirsten tell her about Papa and the milk shop, and the park near the ship where Mama was waiting? How could they understand each other if their words didn't match? Hopelessly, Kirsten traced the dust at her feet with her fingertip.

Then she had an idea. If she couldn't talk, maybe a picture could talk for her. Carefully, Kirsten outlined the shape of the *Eagle* in the dust. Then she drew two big sails over the ship. She pulled at the corner of the woman's apron and pointed to her drawing.

The woman smiled when she saw the picture.

Quickly, she locked her door, put the key in her apron pocket, and motioned for Kirsten to follow her. At the end of the street, they turned into a smaller lane. After a few more turns, they were beside the river, where the ships were docked.

Far ahead, Kirsten could see the tall oak trees of Battery Park. And there was the *Eagle,* tied to the dock. Kirsten ran. She saw the path leading into the park. And at the top of the path, she saw Mama and Papa!

"Mama! Papa! Here I am!" Kirsten shouted.

Mama turned and shaded her eyes to look. Papa began to run down the path, his boots scattering gravel. Kirsten flung herself first into Papa's arms, then into Mama's.

"Kirsten, you frightened us!" Papa said. "We couldn't find you anywhere!"

"I thought you would leave New York without me," Kirsten whispered against Mama's neck. Mama's shoulder smelled wonderfully of soap and dry grass. The sun made her hair look like gold.

"What?" Mama said. "We would never, never leave you! But how did you find your way back?"

Kirsten realized that the kind woman was gone. She pointed to her, walking away along the path beside the river. "I drew a picture of our ship and that American lady helped me find it."

Papa hugged Kirsten again. "You're a very

smart girl," he told her. "Be smart enough to stay right beside me the next time. Promise?"

"I promise!" Kirsten said, and meant it with all her heart.

# ACROSS THE NEW LAND

The next day Kirsten and her family started the long journey across the country to Minnesota. Not even Papa could guess how long the trip would take. "The agent will help us find our way, and we'll see what happens," he said.

At the top of the path into the park, Kirsten met Marta. "We're leaving today," Kirsten said. "Are you going, too?"

Marta shook her head. "Not until tomorrow," she replied.

"Oh, no! I was so sure we'd be traveling together!" exclaimed Kirsten.

"Me, too," Marta answered softly. "Are you

going to take another ship now, Kirsten?"

"No, I think we're going to take a train," Kirsten said. "What do you think a train looks like, Marta?"

"I don't know exactly. My father says it will make a loud noise and a lot of smoke. We might be afraid of trains," Marta said.

Kirsten grinned. "Noise won't hurt us!" she said. "And Papa says a train is like many wagons all traveling together. Maybe you'll get on our train tomorrow. Wouldn't that be lucky?"

Marta caught her lower lip between her teeth. "Or maybe we won't ever see each other again," she said.

Kirsten took her friend's hand. "But your family is going to Minnesota, just like mine is. We're sure to meet on the way. At least, I hope so," she added.

"I'll miss you, Kirsten," Marta murmured.

Kirsten looked down at her dusty boots. Saying good-bye to the people she loved was the hardest thing in the world to do. She didn't want Marta to see the tears that stung her eyes. So she took a deep breath before she said, "Marta, I'll tell you what my grandmother said to me when we left Sweden.

Mormor said, 'When you're lonely, look at the sun. Remember that we all see the same sun.'"

"Do you do that?" Marta asked. "Do you look at the sun and think of your grandmother?"

"When I miss Mormor, I look at the sun and pray for her," Kirsten said.

Now Marta managed a small smile. "Then when I miss you, I'll look at the sun. Will you do the same?"

"Yes. And say a prayer. I will. I'll say, 'God bless Marta.'"

"I'll say a prayer, too," Marta agreed. "And I'll be looking for you everywhere."

Kirsten sighed. She was going to another new place. It seemed to her she would always feel like a Swedish girl who was far from home. Home—that's a place where you're happy, a place where you belong. *How can America ever really be my home?* she thought. Then she followed her parents down the path to meet the agent and ten new families.

First there was a fierce roar and a hiss, then the long scream of a whistle. Kirsten's heart flip-flopped. Maybe Marta was right to be afraid of trains. The engine looked like a black iron house on fire. Smoke boiled up from the giant smokestack. Live sparks and red coals showered down with the smoke. Kirsten stayed close to Mama. But Mama was worried, too. She squeezed Kirsten's hand extra hard as they climbed aboard.

Inside, the train was so hot it felt ready to explode. There was coal grit on the floor and cinders in the air. Kirsten could hardly get her breath. She saw that the windows had been nailed shut. The agent said the train would be safer this way.

Papa and Lars stood near the door. Kirsten was squeezed beside Mama and Peter on a bench under the windows. Trunks and bundles were piled up in front of them. Kirsten was used to being crowded, but now she felt as if she were packed up inside their big painted trunk.

"Aren't we there yet?" Peter complained.

"Hush, we haven't even started to move," Mama said.

Some of the old folks closed their eyes, and Kirsten knew they were praying that the train wouldn't catch on fire. Then it began to move. It bumped and lurched and screeched over the metal rails. Peter hid his face in Mama's lap. The men were quiet, and even Lars's eyes were wide. The train began to huff and chug. Through the small window, Kirsten saw houses and trees moving backward. The huffing and chugging grew louder, and the trees went by very quickly. Lars called out, "We're going faster than a horse can run! Faster than the fastest horse can run!" Dizzy, Kirsten closed her eyes. The train groaned and swayed. Even though she couldn't see, she felt the speed with which it carried them west.

For days, the train traveled through fields and forests. When they stopped for water, a man from the railroad opened the door for a few minutes, but the air stayed hot and hard to breathe. Everyone was quiet, dazed by the heat. Now and then Mama opened the food trunk, but not even Lars was very hungry. When Kirsten caught his eye, he gave her a sad smile. She knew he hated to be trapped inside even more than she did.

At last they reached Chicago. A hot strong wind blew dirt up from the streets, but Kirsten didn't care how dirty it was. Here she could walk again, and run! Papa said that in a few days they would join a big group of pioneers traveling to the Mississippi River in wagons. But first they would rest here, in a boarding house.

It was good to be in a house again, although this boarding house reminded Kirsten of their big barn in Sweden. The long, open sleeping room upstairs was like the loft where Papa stored hay, except it was filled with row after row of beds and crowded with people's belongings. In the kitchen there were big tubs for Mama to wash their clothes in. When the laundry was finished, Mama sent Kirsten and Peter out into the back yard to get some sun. Kirsten found herself on a long porch filled with children. She was used to smiling at other girls, wishing she spoke their language so that they could talk to each other. But now she

*"You're here! You're here!"*
*Kirsten repeated over and over.*

heard someone call her name: "Kirsten Larson!"

It was Marta! Her thick braid swinging, she ran from between the rows of shirts and underwear drying on the clotheslines. She grabbed Kirsten's shoulders, Kirsten grabbed Marta's waist, and they whirled and whirled.

"You're here! You're here!" Kirsten repeated over and over.

"So are you!" Marta answered, again and again.

That evening, Marta's family sat down with Kirsten's family for roast pork and potatoes. Marta's father said, "We're back with our friends again. We'll stay together now until we get to Minnesota." Under the table Kirsten and Marta held hands. Kirsten couldn't believe her good luck. At last America was beginning to feel like home—with good food, a real bed to sleep in, and best of all, friends.

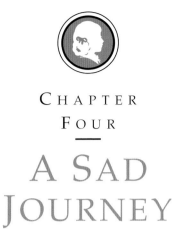

# A SAD
# JOURNEY

Kirsten liked the Mississippi riverboat
the moment she saw it. It was white,
with a pair of wings painted in bright
red on the sides. The boat was named *The Redwing*,
like the red-winged blackbirds that called to one
another along the riverbank. *The Redwing* had broad
decks and a big paddle wheel.

Right away Kirsten wanted to run upstairs to
the wide upper deck. She grabbed Marta's hand,
ducked under a rope, and skipped up the steps. But
before they were to the top step a sailor stopped
them. They didn't understand his words, but they
knew his gesture meant "Get down!"

That evening as they ate their meal of dried

pork and bread, Kirsten asked Papa, "Why can't we go up on the big deck? No one is out there."

"That deck is for rich people," Papa said.

"If we paid more money could we go up there?" asked Kirsten.

Papa rubbed his forehead. "We only have a little money left, Kirsten. And when we leave this boat we'll still have to hire a wagon to reach Olav's farm."

"You've managed our money well," Mama said to Papa. To Kirsten she said crossly, "Don't ask for so much!"

Kirsten was surprised. Mama never talked harshly to her. Why was she cross now? Their long trip was almost over. In a few days they would be at Uncle Olav's.

Kirsten looked closely at her mother. "What's wrong, Mama?" she asked.

Mama said softly, "I'm cross because I'm worried. As we boarded the boat, the sailors were burying a passenger who died of cholera."

"Don't worry so," Lars said to Mama. "We won't get sick! Look at us. We're healthy."

Lars was right. They were strong from walking

beside the wagons on the way to the river and tan from the prairie sun. But Mama didn't smile. "Cholera kills strong ones just like weak ones," she said. "Pray to God that we get safely to Uncle Olav's."

For two days, Kirsten and Marta played together on the riverboat. They watched the hawks circling overhead and counted the fish that jumped from the water. But the third morning, Marta wasn't on the small deck where they were allowed to walk. Marta's father was there alone. He stood at the railing, staring straight ahead at the wide, brown river.

"Where's Marta?" Kirsten asked him.

"Our Marta's very sick," he said. He gripped the railing so tightly that his knuckles were white. "With cholera."

Kirsten's head buzzed. Cholera! Last night after supper, Marta had played with her right here on deck. Last night Marta was perfectly fine. She *couldn't* have cholera now.

"How can she be sick?" Kirsten asked. "She was well yesterday."

"During the night she doubled up with a pain

in her belly. Now she aches and moans and burns with a fever. The captain made us take her to the sick bay," he said.

"Can I go see her?"

Marta's father took Kirsten's wrist firmly. "No, Kirsten. You mustn't. You could get sick, too. Marta's mother is with her. That's all we can do."

But Kirsten had to see Marta. She ran down below the decks, to the part of the boat called the sick bay. Marta was there, lying on a straw mat near the entrance. Her knees were drawn up to her chest. Her mouth was open as though she couldn't breathe. When her mother tried to wipe her forehead, Marta trembled and moaned. Her lips were dry and cracked and her eyelids fluttered.

"Marta," Kirsten whispered. She took a step toward her friend, but Marta's mother sent her away. "Go back to your family, Kirsten. It's dangerous for you here. Marta will get better, you'll see."

Still, Kirsten stayed near the sick bay until Mama found her. "I've looked everywhere for you!" Mama said. "There's nothing we can do for Marta. Not with cholera. You must take care of yourself,

Kirsten! Stay close to me and Papa, please."

So Kirsten stayed close to Mama, but her thoughts were with her sick friend. She told herself that Marta would get well. Over and over she said, *She must get well!*

Kirsten wasn't able to eat, and that night she was sure she would never sleep. But she fell into a restless doze. Later, she woke up with a start. Something was terribly wrong, but in her sleep she'd forgotten what it could be. Then she remembered Marta.

Kirsten ran down to the sick bay. Through the

parted curtains she saw that Marta was gone. *She's better then*, Kirsten thought. She ran up to the deck to find her friend.

The sun was just rising. The riverboat was anchored at a sandy beach below tall bluffs. A gangplank had been lowered for some sailors, who carried a wooden box on their shoulders. They walked along the shore.

Marta's father stood at the railing where Kirsten had seen him last. His arm was around Marta's mother.

Kirsten grabbed Marta's father's sleeve. "Where's Marta?" she asked.

He pointed to the sailors with their box. "Our Marta died last night, Kirsten. The sailors will bury her here. Her soul is in heaven." Then he hid his face in his hand.

"She can't be dead!" Kirsten cried. "She can't be!" Kirsten felt as though her heart was ripped in two. She heard deep sobs that hardly seemed her own. They filled up her chest. She tried to say her friend's name, but her lips wouldn't form the words.

Then Kirsten felt Mama's arms around her,

*Mama cradled her and said softly,*
*"Let her have her tears."*

and Papa patted her shoulder. "Enough crying. Stop now, Kirsten," he said.

But Mama cradled her and said softly, "Let her have her tears."

# HOME AT LAST

It was raining when the Larsons left *The Redwing.* Kirsten didn't watch the riverboat pull away from the dock. She didn't ever want to see that boat again, because Marta had died on it. She was lonely for Marta, and there wasn't any sun in Minnesota to look at with a prayer. So Kirsten looked at the town of Riverton. She saw wet houses, wet trees, and wet horses pulling wagons loaded with wet logs. She blinked into the rain. "God bless you, Marta," she whispered.

Mama touched her cheek. "Cheer up, Kirsten! When Papa and the boys come back with a wagon, it will only take a few hours to reach Olav's farm."

41

But Papa frowned with worry when he strode back to the dock where Kirsten and Mama waited. "We don't have enough money left to rent a horse and wagon," he said.

Mama's shoulders slumped. "What will we do?" she asked.

Papa made his voice strong. "We have our good legs. We'll walk to Olav's farm. We'll just have to leave the trunks here."

Mama looked first at the big painted trunk that held their most precious things, then at the black food trunk with Papa's name lettered on its side. "Everything we own in the world is in these trunks," she said sadly. "How can we get along without our clothes and your tools?"

"We'll take what we can carry now, and we'll have the trunks shipped later," Papa said. "Don't lose heart." He began taking blankets and tools from the big trunk.

After a moment, Mama said, "It can't be helped. We'll send for them soon. People are more important than things, and we're all together and well, thank God." She made a bundle of the bread and cheese that was left, then closed the food trunk.

Papa said, "We need everyone's hands today. Kirsten, you must put your doll here with the other things. You can get her again when the trunks are shipped to us."

Kirsten knew she couldn't say no to Papa. Gently, she put Sari on top of the sweaters and linens in the painted trunk. Before Papa closed the top, she kissed Sari's faded cheek. "You'll be with me soon," she whispered. Then Papa fastened the lock, and he and Lars dragged the trunks to the warehouse.

The family followed Papa down the road along

the river, past tiny houses built of split logs. Everyone carried a bundle, and they walked for hours.
Kirsten's boots were heavy with mud. Her wool skirt
was soaked through to her petticoat. Sometimes she
heard a cow moo, but there were long stretches of
forest or prairie between farms. Even Lars was tired
now. He walked with his head down, his long hair
plastered to his neck by the rain.

By afternoon the rain stopped. The sky was a
smooth, blue bowl. Meadowlarks flew up from the
fields, and daisies and black-eyed Susans bloomed
beside the road. The Larsons were a long, long way
from town when they stopped to eat lunch.

"Olav wrote us the truth," Papa said. "The soil
here is good. We'll have a better life." Before they
walked on, Kirsten picked a daisy for Mama to wear
at her collar.

Now Papa asked the way at each farm they
passed. At last he said, "The next one is Olav's!"
In the distance, Kirsten could see a house, a large

 barn, and a tiny cabin. Cows ambled
down the field toward the barn to be
milked. Smoke rose from the chimney
of the house.

Lars and Peter began to run, splashing through puddles. Lars shouted, "Hello!" and Peter cried, "We're here! We're here!"

A man with a smile like Papa's came from the barn. Two girls and a woman ran from the house. They waved and called out, "Hello! Hello! It's you! At last!"

Suddenly Kirsten was shy. She shrank back behind Mama. Then she heard her own name above the shouts and laughter. "Kirsten? You must be Kirsten!"

The taller girl, who had brown braids and gray eyes, took the heavy bundle from Kirsten's arms. "I'm Lisbeth! I've watched for you every single day."

The little girl with rosy cheeks crowded in. "I've watched, too! I'm Anna!"

Everyone was hugging. Aunt Inger tried to get all the children into her arms at the same time. Papa and Uncle Olav pounded each other's shoulders. Uncle Olav grabbed Lars, then lifted Peter off his feet. Mama cried. Aunt Inger cried. Then they started hugging all over again.

Uncle Olav said, "Come see the barn!"

"No, you don't!" Aunt Inger said. Her smiling

*"Hello! Hello!
It's you! At last!"*

46

face was flushed and red. "First we'll have supper. They're tired and hungry, Olav! They've come halfway around the world to get here."

"And we walked all day long!" Peter added.

Aunt Inger hugged Peter again. Then she turned to Mama and Papa. "You can get settled in your cabin after supper," she said. "And *tomorrow* you men can look at the barn while we women talk. Now come in and eat!"

From the doorway, Kirsten saw fresh bread and butter, a big bowl of potatoes and onions, and a platter of fresh fish on Aunt Inger's long wooden table. Her mouth watered when she noticed a berry tart cooling on the back of the stove.

"Don't worry about a little mud," Aunt Inger said as they began taking off their boots. Then she saw that their clothes were wet, too. "But look how you're soaked through!" she added. "You'll catch cold. We'll find you all some dry things right now." She bustled to a painted trunk like the one Kirsten's family had left in Riverton. From the trunk she took men's brown trousers and white shirts, a blue cotton dress for Mama, and another one for Kirsten.

47

"This was Lisbeth's, but she's outgrown it. It will do for now," Aunt Inger said. "Go put it on and come right down for supper."

Kirsten followed Lisbeth and Anna up the ladder to their place in the loft. Anna gave her a piece of worn quilt to dry her wet arms and legs. "Tomorrow we'll show you our secret fort," she said. "Lisbeth and I play there with our dolls."

"We'll tell you all about it later," Lisbeth added as she handed Kirsten a petticoat. "But let's hurry now. We're hungry, and I bet you are, too."

The dress from Aunt Inger was patterned with little red flowers. Kirsten pulled the soft cotton over her head and Lisbeth did up the buttons. Now Kirsten was dressed just like her cousins. She followed them down the ladder into the cozy kitchen.

When Aunt Inger saw Kirsten, she laughed and pretended to be surprised. "Who's this new girl?" she asked. "Have I met her before?"

Mama took Kirsten's hand and turned her around for a good look. "Why, don't you recognize Kirsten Larson, my American daughter?"

48

The next morning, Kirsten woke up in her very own bed in a small log cabin on Uncle Olav's farm. The cabin was made of split logs. It had a bare plank floor, a small fireplace, and one tiny window. Through the window, Kirsten could see a maple tree. *I'm home,* she thought. *My cousins live right next door. We'll be friends.*

The morning sun was already hot and grasshoppers jumped in the long grass when Lisbeth and Anna led Kirsten down the path toward the stream. "You didn't tell your brothers about our fort, did you?" Anna asked. "Our fort is only for girls!"

Anna's cheerful, round face made Kirsten smile. "No, Anna, I didn't tell them about the fort. I can keep a secret, I promise," she said.

"Oh, good!" Anna carried her rag doll under her arm. The doll's smiling, painted face made Kirsten miss Sari all over again.

Lisbeth held up her hand for them to stop walking. "Is anyone coming?" she asked Anna.

Anna scampered back a few steps and looked down the path they followed through the woods.

49

"No one's coming. We're alone."

"Follow me, then," Lisbeth told Kirsten. She lifted up a pine branch and stepped off the trail into the woods. A carpet of sweet-smelling pine needles covered the ground under the trees.

"We go to our fort through the pines so we won't leave footprints," Anna explained. "We don't want anyone to know where we are."

"Here's the entrance," Lisbeth said. She went down on her knees and crawled into a tunnel made by sumac branches. Kirsten tucked up the skirt of her new dress and crawled after her.

The tunnel ended under the green branches of a wild cherry tree. Lisbeth sat back on her heels. "Here's our fort, Kirsten."

Anna pulled off her sunbonnet and hung it from a branch. "Do you like it here?" she asked.

Kirsten looked around. The overhanging branches made a small, cool room under the tree. She let out a long breath. "Oh, yes!" she said.

"Here's where our dolls sleep," Lisbeth said. She laid her doll on a bed made of sticks tied together at the corners with braided grass. "Now, come up to the loft. Hold tightly so you don't fall." She grabbed the lowest limb of the tree and pulled herself up into the branches. Kirsten gave Anna a boost up, then climbed after her onto a strong limb.

"Here's where we keep a lookout for boys," Anna said, swinging her legs. "Of course we've never seen a boy in the woods, but with Lars and Peter here, we might."

"If we see a boy, we'll get down low and stay quiet," Lisbeth said. "That's one of our rules, Kirsten. Do you promise to keep the rules?"

"I promise to keep all your rules," Kirsten said. She looked out over the trees. When she left Sweden she never imagined she was on her way to a hiding place in a cherry tree.

"Since you live here now, you must have a place in our fort just for your doll," Lisbeth said.

"Choose where!" Anna insisted.

Kirsten peered down through the branches into the fort below. "There," Kirsten said, and she pointed to a

*"Since you live here now, you
must have a place in our fort,"* Lisbeth said.

moss-covered spot. She scooted down the tree and patted the moss. It was soft and cool. Oh, Sari would like it here!

Anna climbed down, too. She got her doll and walked her across the fort to Sari's spot. "I'm coming to visit," she made her doll say. "Where is Sari?"

"Sari's still on her way," Kirsten answered. "But come visit me! *I'm* here!"

FOR MY MOTHER,
NADINA FOWLER

# 1854
# KIRSTEN
# LEARNS
# A LESSON
## *A School Story*

# MISS WINSTON

*tine*

Kirsten hurried down the path beside her cousin Lisbeth. In one hand she carried a lunch in her wooden tine. With the other she held her shawl tightly around her shoulders.

"You're walking too fast!" Kirsten said.

But Lisbeth didn't slow down. "Mr. Coogan will be angry if we're late. He's really strict," she answered. Lisbeth was eleven. Mr. Coogan had been her teacher since she was nine. She loved to tell stories about how fierce he was. In fact ever since July, when Kirsten and her family had come to live on Uncle Olav's farm, Lisbeth and her sister Anna had talked about Mr. Coogan and Powderkeg

School. Now it was November. The harvest was over and it was time for the fall term to begin. Today would be Kirsten's first day in an American school.

Kirsten walked as fast as she could to keep up with Lisbeth's longer stride. Her boots puffed up dust.

Anna, who was just seven, tagged farther behind. "Wait for me," she called. "I want to stop for a drink of water."

Kirsten and Lisbeth stopped beside the stream. A light mist rose from the clear water, and a few yellow leaves floated on it. Kirsten stopped and put her fingertip into a deer track in the sand. How she wished she could stay here by the stream instead of going to school.

"If you mind him, Mr. Coogan will like you," Lisbeth said. "But he gets really angry when the big boys fight."

"In Sweden the boys weren't allowed to fight in school," Kirsten said.

Lisbeth smiled and tossed her head. "Well, this

is America, and here the boys get wild whether they should or not. Sometimes Mr. Coogan hits them with a cane. Once he punched Amos Anderson with his fist! If you talk back to Mr. Coogan, he swats your hand with his ruler."

Anna wiped her mouth on the back of her hand. Her round cheeks were rosy from running along the path. "He's mean! But he'll never hit you, Kirsten. You're too nice. Don't worry."

Kirsten let out a long breath. "I'm not really worried," she said softly. But she was dizzy, the way she'd felt on the ship just before she was seasick.

"Does your stomach hurt?" Anna asked. "When I'm scared, my stomach hurts and flutters like there's a bird inside me."

Kirsten put her hand to her waist. Yes, her stomach did feel full of wings. Butterflies, maybe. And she hadn't been able to eat the pancakes Mama made for breakfast. "My stomach hurts a little," she admitted.

"I was really scared the first day I went to school," Anna said. "I wondered if the others would like me. It's hard to be the new girl."

Lisbeth slipped her arm through Kirsten's as

they started along the path again. "Just do what we do, Kirsten. You'll get along fine in school."

Kirsten sighed. "But I can't do what you do. I only speak a little bit of English, and I can't read a word of it. I won't fit in at all." How she wished she were back in her village in Sweden, where she knew everyone and everyone knew her and they all spoke the same language.

"School only lasts until four o'clock," Anna added. "When it's over, we can stop at our fort and play for a few minutes." She darted off to hide their dolls in the secret hideaway under the cherry tree. On her way back, she broke off a sprig of bittersweet and handed Kirsten a few of the waxy red berries.

"We can put these berries on our doll cakes," Kirsten said.

"Come on!" Lisbeth said. "I hear the school bell." She began to run.

And suddenly, before Kirsten was ready, they were in the clearing in front of the large log cabin that was Powderkeg School. The last children were just going in the door.

Powderkeg School didn't look very different

from the log cabin Kirsten and her
family lived in on Uncle Olav's farm.
But the school had more windows,
and a stovepipe stuck up in the
center of the roof.

"There's the outhouse," Anna said. She pointed
to a small shed behind the log cabin. "Girls use it
before boys do at recess. I won't let any boys peek
at you, I promise."

Kirsten hadn't thought of *that!* What a lot of
things she had to worry about! She peered around
Lisbeth's shoulder into the schoolhouse. Children
were finding places to sit on the benches that lined
the walls. Only her brothers, Lars and Peter, looked
familiar. Lars sat with the other big boys. Peter was
with the younger boys, some even smaller than he.

Kirsten took a deep breath, as though she were
about to dive into the stream. She followed Anna
and Lisbeth through the door.

Lisbeth pulled off her shawl and hung it on a
peg. Kirsten draped hers over it. For a moment she
let her forehead rest against the comforting wool
that smelled of woodsmoke. Then she turned and
looked around.

A pot-bellied wood stove sat in the open space in the center of the room. But instead of the fearsome Mr. Coogan, a young woman in a black dress sat on the teacher's chair by the stove. She watched Kirsten and her cousins as they walked to the benches on the girls' side of the room. But she didn't smile a welcome.

"We have a new teacher," Lisbeth whispered as she and Kirsten sat down.

The young teacher stood and tapped the stove with a ruler to get everyone's attention. Her dark hair was parted cleanly in the middle, her chin was up, her shoulders were back like a soldier's. "I am Miss Winston," she said in a crisp voice. "I've come west from Camden, Maine. I'm to be your teacher because Mr. Coogan was injured when his horse threw him." She looked around to see if all the students had heard her.

"I hope his horse stepped on him, too!" a black-haired boy said out loud.

"That's Amos Anderson!" Lisbeth whispered.

Miss Winston faced Amos. "You will not talk out of turn in my classroom. Although we live in the woods, we are not savages like the Indians."

*"You will not talk out of turn in my classroom,"*
*Miss Winston said.*

Amos grinned and looked down at his big hands. He had broad shoulders and the beginnings of a black mustache. Kirsten thought he looked more like a man than a boy.

"Now you know my name," Miss Winston continued. "But I don't know yours. I'd like each of you to come forward and introduce yourself to me politely. We are ladies and gentlemen here at Powderkeg School."

Anna was the first of the girls to go forward. She made a quick curtsy and said, "Anna Larson, ma'am."

Miss Winston nodded. "Very good. Next, please."

Kirsten tried to remember the names of the girls, but her head buzzed like a hive of bees. She didn't want to walk out there in the middle of the room with everyone watching her. She was the last girl to take her turn. The floor seemed to move under her as she stepped forward. She kept her gaze on her dusty boots as she made her curtsy.

"Kirsten Larson," she muttered.

Before she could escape back to the bench, Miss Winston said firmly, "Say 'Kirsten Larson, *ma'am.*'"

"Ma'am," Kirsten repeated. But the word didn't sound right. She felt a blush prickle at the base of her throat.

Miss Winston bent to look Kirsten right in the eye. "Do you speak English?" she asked.

"A little, ma'am." The buzz in Kirsten's ears was so loud she could hardly hear her own words. But she heard one of the girls giggle at her halting English.

"She's our cousin, Miss Winston!" Anna said. "She came to America last summer. We speak Swedish at home, ma'am."

Miss Winston raised her eyebrows and said, "Ah! Well, you will speak English in school, Kirsten. And you will begin with the easiest lessons. Anna will share her book with you and help you. Do you understand?"

Kirsten nodded.

"Say, 'I understand, ma'am,'" Miss Winston reminded her. "If you're going to learn English, you must practice. Practice makes perfect."

Now it was Amos who laughed at Kirsten.

Miss Winston's eyes narrowed, and she motioned for Kirsten to sit down again on the bench.

Then Miss Winston whirled around, raised her ruler over her head, and brought it smashing down on the top of the iron stove. The crack went through the room like the shot of a rifle.

"My father could not be a ship's captain if he weren't in charge of his crew. I couldn't be a teacher if I weren't in charge of my students." Again she raised the ruler high and smacked the stove. "This is your first lesson," she said. "'Miss Winston hit the stove.' *Miss Winston* is the subject of that sentence. *Hit* is the verb. The direct object of *hit* is *the stove.* Be careful that the direct object of *hit* isn't *the student.* Do you have any questions?"

No one said a single thing.

"Good. Now, you boys please come and introduce yourselves. Remember, you are gentlemen, not savages."

The littlest boys went first. They spoke their names and bowed. Even Peter, who was only five, took his turn easily. He'd learned a lot of English without even seeming to try, Kirsten thought.

It was Lars's turn. He said, "I'm Lars Larson,

ma'am," in a loud voice that everyone could hear easily. Lars wasn't afraid of anything, not even this teacher who seemed so strict. Mama had cut his hair last night, and it hugged his head like a bright cap.

Amos, with his dark mustache and eyes the color of blue paint, came last. He was much taller than Miss Winston. He looked as tall as Uncle Olav. "Amos Anderson, *ma'am*," he said. He bobbed his head instead of bowing.

"Which reading book are you using, Amos?" Miss Winston asked him.

"I finished the third one, *ma'am*." He winked at the girls' bench.

"Only the third? How old are you?" Miss Winston asked.

"I'm nineteen," Amos drawled. "Same as you."

Miss Winston tapped her palm with her ruler and considered him. "Yes, Amos, I am nineteen too. But I am the teacher and you are the student. I'm here to help you read and do sums the way a man must if he wants to make his way in the world. Please set a good example for the others."

Amos's face turned red. He looked at Miss

Winston closely. "Why don't I go draw a bucket of water so that the children can all have a drink before we start in reading," he said.

"Thank you, Amos. That's a good idea," Miss Winston said. Amos grabbed one of the wooden buckets. Through the small window, Kirsten saw him run like a deer toward the stream.

Miss Winston stood with her back to the door. "While we wait for our drink of water, we'll sing a song. Singing is very good exercise. It brings fresh air into our lungs." Keeping time with her ruler, she sang,

> "Be it ever so humble,
> There's no place like home."

Her voice was firm and clear. Everyone sang along.

*Home*—the word was as sweet as clover honey on Kirsten's lips. How she wished she were home in Sweden where she was comfortable, where she could be herself. Or home with Mama, in their cozy cabin. Or anywhere but here with Miss Winston, in Powderkeg School.

Soon the singing stopped, and Amos was back

with the bucket of water. He set it on the bench and handed Anna the dipper so she could get a drink. "Girls first," he said, as though he were in charge here, not Miss Winston. If Miss Winston minded, she didn't show it. She was busy passing out the books, small slates, and slate pencils.

Anna leaned against Kirsten's shoulder and opened her book to the alphabet section. She ran her finger down the page to the picture of a dog. "'D. Dog.' Doesn't this dog look just like our Brownie when he smells a fox?" Anna said. "See, here are the letters that spell 'dog.' Copy them on your slate like I do."

Kirsten took her slate and did as Anna told her to. Once in a while Anna licked her finger, erased one of Kirsten's letters, and had her start again. Kirsten pressed her tongue against her upper lip and tried hard. Around her the other children worked at their reading. Some of them read out loud.

When Miss Winston came to check Kirsten's work, she said, "It seems Anna is a good teacher. Can you read what you've written here?"

"Dog," Kirsten said proudly. She hoped Miss Winston might say she'd done well.

Instead, Miss Winston pointed to Anna's slate. "You must learn to write 'The dog can run,' as Anna has done," she said.

"I love school, don't you?" Anna whispered.

Kirsten glanced up at the dusty windowpanes. It was still early morning. The first day of school was going to be a long one. She sighed and wrote again on her slate.

At last the first day of school was over. On their way home, Kirsten and her cousins stopped to play in their fort under the cherry tree. Anna fetched the dolls she'd hidden that morning.

Anna's and Lisbeth's rag dolls had pretty painted faces. But Kirsten's doll didn't even have a face. It was an outgrown stocking stuffed with milkweed floss. Kirsten's real doll, Sari, was still in the painted trunk they had to store in Riverton. Kirsten missed her Sari so much that she named her sock doll Little Sari.

"Hello, children!" Anna said to the dolls in her high voice. "Come introduce yourselves like ladies!" To Kirsten she said, "Do you think Miss Winston is nice?"

"I don't know," Kirsten said. "She likes you, Anna. I don't think she likes me. And remember how she scolded?"

"Yes, she was fierce," Anna said.

"Is that what Mr. Coogan was like?" Kirsten asked.

"No, he was *much* worse," Lisbeth answered.

"Let's play school," Anna suggested. She patted down the long soft grass and picked out three red sumac leaves for benches. The girls sat their dolls down in a row.

"We'll pretend it's lunchtime," Kirsten said. She thought lunch had been the only good part of the school day. After she had eaten her bread and cheese and sausage, she played tree tag with the others in the school yard. In tag it didn't matter that Kirsten couldn't speak English well, because she was one of the fastest runners.

Now Lisbeth placed a little cake made of dried mud in front of each doll. "Here's your lunch,

children," she said. One mud cake was decorated
with gooseberries, one with acorn caps, one with
sunflower seeds in a star pattern.

Anna clapped her hands and scolded the dolls.
"No, no, children! Don't eat so fast! Remember you
are not savages like the Indians!" She sounded
exactly like Miss Winston.

When Kirsten laughed she lost some of the
flutters that had been in her stomach all day. "What
does 'savage' mean?" she asked Lisbeth.

Lisbeth made a scary face and pretended her
hands were scratching claws. "Savage means wild!"

"Are the Indians really savage?" Kirsten asked.

"Some people say the Indians are kind," Lisbeth said as she gave her doll a second cake. "They say the Indians gave them deer meat and corn when they needed food. But other people say the Indians are cruel and bloodthirsty."

"An Indian came to our door once, when Mama was roasting pork," Anna said. "Mama gave him a piece of meat and he went away."

"He didn't hurt us, but he didn't say 'thank you,' either," Lisbeth said.

"He *looked* savage," Anna said. "He had red paint on his cheeks and eagle feathers in his hair. He didn't wear trousers. And we didn't hear him coming. We looked up and suddenly he was in the doorway." Anna's eyes were wide. "That's Indian magic."

Lisbeth laughed. "That's not magic, Anna. They wear soft shoes, that's all."

"They wear long knives, too," Anna said. She shivered and hugged her doll. "And they live in tents."

"Papa worries about the Indians," Lisbeth said. "He says that if we plant crops on their hunting land the wild animals will go away. He says the Indians won't have enough to eat then, and they'll surely be angry. I don't know . . ." Her voice trailed off and she looked at Kirsten with her gray eyes. "Papa says we need the land, too."

"Do the Indians live in their tents all winter? Don't they get cold?" asked Kirsten.

"I don't know," Lisbeth said. "You're too curious, Kirsten! Let's just play school."

# CHAPTER TWO

## A SECRET FRIEND

A few days later Miss Winston opened class by saying, "I have good news for you today." Her face was flushed and she held her hands behind her back as though she hid a present there. "We are going to do something special in Powderkeg School this year! Each one of you will learn a poem. When you've memorized it, you will stand here by the stove and recite it to your classmates. If you do an excellent job, you'll earn a Reward of Merit."

Kirsten slipped down in her seat. Oh, this was too much. Even if she learned to read a poem, how could she remember it? And if she did manage somehow to remember it, how could she stand

75

there in Miss Winston's place and say the words out loud?

"Just saying your poem is not enough, of course," Miss Winston went on. There was excitement in her voice. "You must speak with feeling! If your poem expresses anger, you must do *this.*" She stretched out her neck and turned down her lips.

A few of the boys tried that, and laughed until she frowned at them.

"If your poem expresses love, you must do *this.*" Now Miss Winston smoothed her forehead, smiled gently, and lowered her eyelids. "There are many feelings to express. This is excellent training for your young minds, believe me."

Kirsten chewed on her knuckle. Flutters had come back into her stomach again.

Miss Winston walked among the students, giving everyone a different poem. When she got to Kirsten, she paged to the back of the first reading book. "Oh, here's a good one for you, Kirsten. It's not too long, and it will give you a chance to show both anger and love. You're a lucky girl!" She pointed to the poem.

To Kirsten the words seemed to swim on the page like tadpoles in the stream. When Miss Winston moved on, Kirsten said, "Quick, Anna, read it to me."

Anna read:

> "Coo, coo, says the gentle dove,
>    Coo, coo, says its little mate;
>    They play with each other in love,
>    And never show anger or hate."

As Anna read, Kirsten tried very hard not to cry. But tears came to her eyes. How could she ever learn all these words? She wished she could just vanish from Powderkeg School like a ghost disappearing into the night.

The next morning, when Kirsten went down to the stream to fetch Mama a bucket of water, a V of geese was flying south. She stopped on the path to watch the geese. Then she stopped again when she came upon a deer drinking at the stream.

She stood very still and waited for the deer to finish drinking. Then she heard a bird's whistle. She looked across the stream. Turtles sunned on a fallen log. A frog jumped into the water. Then, among the cattails, she saw a dark face watching her—dark eyes, black hair, the fringed sleeve of a deerskin dress. An Indian girl stood right there!

Kirsten held her breath. The Indian girl looked at her without blinking.

"Hello," Kirsten said softly.

The Indian girl didn't speak or move. But the word startled the deer away into the pines. When Kirsten looked back from the deer for the Indian girl, she was gone.

Kirsten thought maybe she'd only imagined the girl had been there. Maybe her eyes had played tricks on her. She crossed the stream on the stones and walked a little way into the cattails. No one. But when she went back to the shore, she saw there was a footprint in the soft sand. The footprint was a little smaller than the print left by her own boots. And near the footprint was a blue bead no larger than a gooseberry. The girl must have dropped it.

Kirsten stooped and picked up the bead. She wrapped it in her hankie and put it deep into her apron pocket. As she filled her bucket with water, Kirsten wondered if the girl had been sent here for water, too. Kirsten wanted to meet her. How could she do that? Would the girl come again?

Kirsten had an idea. She set down her bucket, hurried into the woods, and crawled into the fort.

 She took one of the doll cakes decorated with a circle of tiny snail shells. Then she crossed the stream again and laid the doll cake on the sand by the girl's footprints. If the Indian girl came back to the stream, maybe she'd find the doll cake. If she did, she'd know it was Kirsten who left it there.

When Kirsten got back to the cabin, her breakfast waited for her on the table. Mama scolded, "You were gone so long I thought you'd lost your way. Lars and Peter have already left for school. Hurry, or you'll be late."

All day Kirsten wondered about the Indian girl. When Kirsten went back to the stream after supper, the doll cake was gone. In its place was the

green wing feather of a duck, stuck into the sand like a little flag. Kirsten smiled as she picked up the duck feather and put it into her hankie with the bead. Maybe there was a way to make friends with the dark-eyed girl.

Every morning and every evening when she went for water, Kirsten looked for the Indian girl. Kirsten practiced walking very quietly through the woods in the hope that she might surprise her. Maybe the girl hid in the cattails, watching her. Kirsten didn't know exactly when the girl came to the stream, but she knew when she'd been there. Because every time Kirsten left a gift on the shore, the girl took it and left something in its place.

Once Kirsten left a piece of red yarn wrapped around a white pebble. In its place she found a length of leather thong as smooth as silk.

Kirsten left a little doll she'd shaped from mud, with a leaf stuck on for a skirt. That night she found a tiny basket woven of grass where the doll had been.

Kirsten left a green button on a loop of green

thread. It was replaced by a purple bead. Kirsten strung the two beads on the leather thong. She kept them wrapped in her hankie with the feather and the tiny basket. These were her secret treasures, and the Indian girl was her secret friend. At school, when Kirsten was tired of writing and numbers, of trying to learn her poem and trying to please Miss Winston, she daydreamed of running off across the prairie with the Indian girl. They wouldn't need to talk. They'd run faster than the wind.

How Kirsten wanted to see the mysterious girl again! One evening she saved her slice of bread and honey from supper. She wrapped the honey sandwich in oak leaves. Then she went to the stream for water. She put the package of oak leaves on the other shore, then settled down to wait. Maybe the Indian girl came here at dusk. Kirsten decided she would meet her, no matter what.

But the sun was almost down. Kirsten wasn't allowed to stay away from the cabin after sunset—Mama would worry. "Please come," Kirsten whispered under her breath, as though that would make the Indian girl appear.

And then, there she was! In her dress of soft deerskin, the Indian girl slipped silently through the cattails. She stooped and picked up the oak leaf package. She peeled off the leaves, sniffed, and began to eat the bread and honey. As she ate she looked right at Kirsten. Kirsten didn't speak. She didn't want to frighten the girl away again. Instead, she walked slowly forward, watching the girl.

The girl was a little smaller than Kirsten. Her hair and skin shone as if they'd been polished. Kirsten thought she'd never seen eyes so inky black. The Indian girl licked honey from her finger. She watched Kirsten, too.

Dark shadows moved on the stream as Kirsten crossed the stones. When she stood in front of the Indian girl, the girl reached into the leather pouch she wore around her waist. She held out to Kirsten a tiny clay pot decorated with markings that might have been made from a sharp twig.

Kirsten took the little pot. It was as small as an acorn. "It's pretty!" she breathed.

The Indian girl looked at her hard. Slowly, as though she feared she would scare Kirsten, she reached out and touched Kirsten's yellow braid.

*Slowly, the Indian girl*
*reached out and touched Kirsten's yellow braid.*

Then she touched the other one.

Kirsten was so pleased that she laughed. She held out the little pot again and repeated, "Pretty!"

The Indian girl couldn't seem to take her gaze from Kirsten's yellow hair. Again, she stroked one of Kirsten's looped braids.

Kirsten touched the girl's beaded necklace. Oh, if only they could talk to each other! "Pretty," Kirsten said. "Pretty."

The girl's eyes were as unblinking as a deer's. She touched Kirsten's apron, which was decorated with a cross-stitched border. She said something— what was it? "Tee. Pur. Tee."

*She's saying "pretty,"* Kirsten thought. She wished she could take off her apron and give it to the girl. But Mama would be angry if Kirsten came home without her apron. So instead, she took her hankie from her pocket, opened the little bundle, and showed the girl the gifts she'd saved. The girl made a pleased purring sound deep in her throat.

Kirsten put the gifts and the little pot into her apron pocket. She held out her hankie to the girl. The hankie had a cross-stitched border in blue and red— Kirsten had sewed it herself.

"Here, *pretty*," she said.

The Indian girl took the hankie. "Pur-tee," she repeated after Kirsten.

Then Kirsten realized that it was almost night. If she didn't hurry, she wouldn't get back to the cabin before dark. Quickly, Kirsten bent down and drew in the sand. She made a setting sun. Then she pointed to where the red sun was sinking down beyond the trees.

The girl looked at the sun, then at the drawing. She squatted and drew a picture just like Kirsten's in the sand. Now there were two suns side by side.

Kirsten touched each one. "Will you come tomorrow when the sun is like this?" she asked.

The Indian girl only stared at her. She touched the hankie Kirsten had given her to her cheek. Then she turned and was swiftly gone into the cattails along the stream.

# VISITORS

 "Miss Winston's coming to live at our house!" Lisbeth said proudly.

Kirsten was walking to school with Lisbeth and Anna. "Oh, no!" she replied.

"It's an *honor,* Kirsten," Lisbeth said. "We've never had a teacher live with us."

"But we didn't *want* Mr. Coogan," Anna added. She wrapped her shawl more tightly, because the November days were turning colder.

Kirsten's spirits sank. The best part of the school day was when she left Powderkeg School and headed home. If Miss Winston came to Lisbeth and Anna's, it would be as though school followed her home.

But Anna was so excited she skipped. "Won't it be grand! Miss Winston will eat supper with us every night. She'll have a bed up in the loft near ours. Papa hung up a curtain to make her a little room."

Lisbeth laced her arm through Kirsten's. "Miss Winston's been living in a shed off the Engbergs' kitchen, but now the shed is too cold. She says our house will be wonderful. She's heard our mama is a good cook."

"Well, there's no room for her in our cabin," Kirsten said firmly. "Anyway, my mama doesn't speak any English at all." In the chill air her breath made little clouds at her lips.

"But that's the best part!" Anna went on. "You and your family will eat with us more often. Your mama will cook with mine, and we'll all have supper together. That way your mama and papa can learn more English. Papa says that with Miss Winston at the table, it won't be polite to speak Swedish."

Now Kirsten's spirits sank even lower. The happiest time for her family was when they sat down together for supper. Papa talked about the crops and the animals. Mama spoke of the wool she was spinning. She almost had enough to begin weaving. Lars and Peter joked about the pranks the boys played at recess. How could they speak of these things if they struggled with English?

And Kirsten didn't want to have school lessons at suppertime, too. Would Miss Winston smack her ruler on Uncle Olav's table as she did on the stove at school?

"When is she coming?" Kirsten asked.

"Next Sunday," Lisbeth said.

Quickly, Kirsten counted the days. This was Tuesday, so there were only five more nights of freedom left.

"Just think," Anna said, "she'll dress right in our room! I bet she has beautiful petticoats. She's a lady, you know. Ladies wear beautiful underclothes, I'm sure of it."

Kirsten scowled. "Anna, I don't care what kind of underclothes Miss Winston wears!" But when she saw Anna's lower lip tremble, she took her cousin's arm. "I didn't mean to hurt your feelings."

"You're probably cross because you've had

such a hard time remembering your poem," Lisbeth said.

That comment didn't make Kirsten feel any better. She put her hand into her apron pocket, where she kept the gifts Singing Bird had given her. That was the Indian girl's name: Singing Bird. She and Kirsten were already the best of friends. Every day, they'd explore the woods and the caves along the stream. Singing Bird taught Kirsten to whistle like a meadowlark. When Kirsten was with Singing Bird, she felt as free as the rabbits they scattered as they ran. She felt as strong and swift as the young deer they often came upon in the woods. She forgot to worry about trying to fit in at school, about trying to learn her lessons, about trying to speak English correctly.

That afternoon there were long shadows under the pines when Kirsten ran to the stream with the bucket bumping her leg. Singing Bird waited for her under a willow tree.

"Hello!" Kirsten said.

Singing Bird touched Kirsten's blond braid, as she liked to do. "Ho," she said.

Kirsten beckoned for Singing Bird to follow her farther into the woods. For several days, Kirsten had planned to take Singing Bird to the doll fort under the cherry tree. Lisbeth and Anna might be cross if Kirsten took someone into the fort without their permission—especially an Indian. But Kirsten had decided to take a chance.

Singing Bird crawled behind Kirsten through the tunnel into the fort. Red leaves carpeted the ground there. A raccoon peered at the girls from the lowest branch of the cherry tree. The yellowed grass inside the fort was still thick, and all the doll furniture was there.

Singing Bird's eyes grew wide when Kirsten showed her the stacks of doll cakes and cookies. "Purtee!" she said. She touched the three doll beds of woven twigs, the doll blankets woven from scraps of cotton, and the little cross Lisbeth had made so they could pretend their dolls went to church. Kirsten took the tiny basket and clay pot from her pocket. She put them on the table with the doll cakes. She pretended to drink from the pot, then offered it to Singing Bird.

Singing Bird gathered a few bare twigs and tied

them together at one end with a strand of grass. She set the twigs upright on the moss and wrapped a large oak leaf around them. "Tepee," she told Kirsten. Then she walked her fingers into the tepee. "Come," she said.

Kirsten laughed with pleasure. She put the small basket and pot into the tepee. Then she walked her fingers inside, as Singing Bird had done. "Here I am," she said.

Singing Bird shook her head. "*My* tepee." She stood and stretched her arms wide to show Kirsten she spoke of a real tepee.

Kirsten's heart sped up. Singing Bird wanted her to go to the Indian village! Kirsten knew the Indian village was close by, but she didn't know where. Lars said he had seen the tepees when he was out setting traps for rabbits. But none of the children at school had been there. Most of them did not trust Indians. Of course, they didn't know Singing Bird.

"Where is your tepee?" Kirsten asked.

Singing Bird pointed toward the ridge where the sun was setting.

"Yes! I'll come!" Kirsten said.

*"My tepee."*
*Singing Bird stretched her arms wide.*

But she knew that it was too late to go today. Every day the sun set earlier, and the sky was already getting dark now. So she added, "I'll come *soon*." Then she put the doll furniture back in place, and Singing Bird untied the small tepee and scattered the twigs. They walked back to the stream together.

Instead of drawing a setting sun as a promise to meet tomorrow, Singing Bird drew a full sun and pointed to the east. She meant for them to meet in the morning. Kirsten shook her head, then drew two suns like Singing Bird's. She meant she couldn't come tomorrow, but she would be there the next day, before she went to school. She would meet Singing Bird and go to her village. Kirsten didn't know how she'd get away, but she knew she would.

Then, as she could do so easily, Singing Bird vanished into the shadowy grove and was gone.

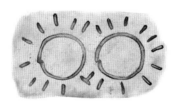

93

# SINGING BIRD
# AND YELLOW HAIR

Miss Winston stopped next to Kirsten's seat and tapped the back of the log bench with her ruler. "I don't believe you're really *trying*," the teacher scolded. "Why can't you learn your poem?"

Kirsten bit her lip. "I *am* trying, ma'am," she said.

"Please look at me when I speak to you," Miss Winston said.

Kirsten forced herself to look up. She thought that if Miss Winston didn't look so stern she would be very pretty.

"Can you *read* the words of your poem?" Miss Winston asked. She pointed to the lines which

Kirsten had been trying all week to memorize.

"I can read the words, but I can't remember them," Kirsten murmured.

"Your cousin Lisbeth recited all thirty-two lines of 'To a Waterfowl.' I'm only asking you to memorize these few lines. Your memory is like a muscle, Kirsten. You must use it to make it strong."

Kirsten nodded unhappily. Her poor mind felt like a tired muscle. When she tried to say her poem without looking at the book, the words seemed to disappear like geese flying into the mist.

It seemed everyone could memorize and recite except Kirsten. Amos Anderson had learned a whole poem. He recited it with his voice galloping along like the horses and the battle he described. Miss Winston had smiled proudly when she handed him a Reward of Merit. Kirsten thought that Miss Winston was proud of everyone but her.

"You *must* try harder," Miss Winston said firmly. "If at first you don't succeed, try, try again."

Kirsten thought that even if she could memorize her poem, she was sure to forget it when she stood up in front of the class. If she forgot, she might cry. That would be the worst thing of all.

The next morning, Kirsten got up extra early and rushed through her chores. "Why are you in such a hurry?" Mama asked. She put out several thin pancakes and a slice of ham for Kirsten's breakfast.

Kirsten wrapped the ham in a pancake. "I'll eat on the way to school. I'm going early to practice saying my verse."

"You've learned a verse in English? Oh, you're a smart girl, Kirsten," Mama said with a big smile.

"Go on, then, if you're doing schoolwork," Papa said.

Kirsten ran for the door. "Tell Lisbeth and Anna I'm practicing. I'll meet them at school," she said. She knew it was wrong to lie to Mama and Papa, but she couldn't help herself. As she ran to meet Singing Bird she *tried* to say her poem so the lie wouldn't be such a bad one.

As soon as she heard Singing Bird whistle, Kirsten forgot all about the poem and her lie. She

handed Singing Bird the pancake and the meat, and the girl ate gladly. Then Singing Bird said, "Come."

Kirsten ran behind Singing Bird through the long, pale prairie grass. Crows flew up beside them, and rabbits scattered. Kirsten didn't even care how far they had to run. She was glad to be free from school, glad to be on this adventure with Singing Bird.

They ran through a grove of pines, then up a trail to the top of a hill. Down below, five big Indian tepees circled a large campfire. Nearby, spotted ponies grazed.

As the girls started down the hill to the village, scrawny Indian dogs ran barking to meet them. Then Indian children came from the tepees. They spoke to Singing Bird in their language.

The children crowded around and wanted to touch Kirsten's blond hair. One little boy crouched to touch her leather boots and their laces. Indian women came forward to look at Kirsten's apron, too. Their dark hands were gentle.

Singing Bird stood close by Kirsten's side. Then she said, "Come. Come to my father," and pointed to the tallest tepee.

Kirsten followed Singing Bird to the tepee. It was made of buffalo skins. Singing Bird lifted the flap that was its door. Inside, the tepee was dim and warm. When Kirsten's eyes adjusted to the gloom, she saw a man sitting cross-legged on a bear skin. Eagle feathers were braided into his hair, and he wore a necklace of bear claws.

"I am Brave Elk," he said in a deep voice.

"How do you do," Kirsten said, and remembered to curtsy.

"You are Singing Bird's friend," he said.

"Yes," Kirsten said. She touched Singing Bird's

arm to make sure she was at her side. "Singing Bird is my friend, too."

"You teach your English words to Singing Bird," Brave Elk said.

"My English words?" That surprised Kirsten. But she thought Brave Elk was right—she hadn't once thought of trying to speak Swedish with Singing Bird. "Singing Bird teaches me, too," Kirsten went on. "Tepee. Moccasin." She pointed to those things to show Brave Elk she knew what she said in his language.

The chief nodded. "Good. You are Yellow Hair. You are welcome here. You stay," he said.

He motioned to the woman who stood in the shadows. The woman gave Kirsten a piece of flat bread made from cornmeal.

Now Singing Bird led Kirsten to sit beside her on a pile of animal skins. She showed Kirsten her leather pouch which held a knife, a bone needle, and a length of sinew for sewing. She showed Kirsten her doll, which was made of soft buckskin and stuffed with grass.

Oh, how Kirsten wished she could live here in

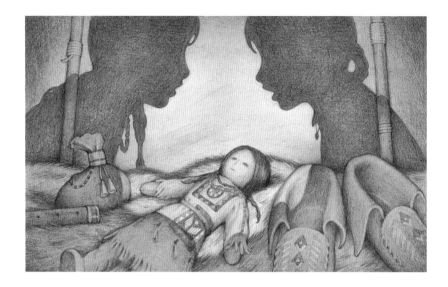

this warm tent with Singing Bird. She would wear soft moccasins like Singing Bird's. She would wear a deerskin dress and leggings. She would sleep under warm buffalo hides and play with a little buckskin doll of her own. All day she and Singing Bird would play in the fields and woods. Instead of Kirsten Larson, who couldn't memorize her poem, she would be Yellow Hair, Singing Bird's sister.

A little boy came into the tepee to show Kirsten his wooden top. When he lifted the tent flap, Kirsten saw that the sun had risen high in the sky. She would have to run fast in order to get to school on time. She touched Singing Bird's arm and pointed to the sun. The girl said something to her father, then held open the tent flap. "Come," she said to Kirsten. And they ran back up the trail.

# BELONGING

 It was Sunday night, and Miss Winston sat next to Uncle Olav at the table. It was her first meal with the Larsons.

Aunt Inger and Mama had made a big dinner to welcome her. They'd even baked ginger cookies, just like at Christmas.

"My parents have a lovely home on a harbor in Maine," Miss Winston said. "There's a small room on the top. It has windows on all four sides. When my father is at sea, we watch for his ship from that room."

"What a fine room that must be!" Anna said. She was the only one talking to Miss Winston.

Uncle Olav offered everyone more rabbit stew.

Mama kept busy cutting and passing bread.

"Why did you want to leave such a lovely home?" Anna asked. She was so excited to have Miss Winston there that she'd forgotten all about her supper.

"Well, I certainly wasn't ready to marry and spend the rest of my life in a house," Miss Winston said. "I wanted to travel, to meet people, to have adventures! School-teachers travel, so I decided to become a teacher. Maybe you will be a teacher when you grow up, Anna. You've been a good little teacher for Kirsten."

Kirsten kept her eyes on her tin plate. With Miss Winston at the table, it seemed she'd forgotten all the English she'd ever learned. And what if Mama or Papa said something to Miss Winston about the poem Kirsten said she had memorized? Miss Winston would say Kirsten hadn't done it. Kirsten's head ached at the thought.

Anna said, "Does your father sail on his ship every day?"

Miss Winston smiled. "No, Anna, he isn't a fisherman. He has a big ship for carrying heavy cargo. He sails down the coast with a load of wool. Then he sails back with a load of tobacco."

"I might want to be a sailor," Lars said. "Life is exciting on a ship!"

Miss Winston looked at Lars. "Would you like to see my father's ship?"

"*Ja!*" Lars said. Then he reddened and corrected himself. "Yes, ma'am."

"Then after our meal, I'll show you a surprise," Miss Winston said.

"Eat, Anna," Uncle Olav commanded. "You'll get thin if you don't pay attention to your dinner."

After everyone had finished eating, Miss Winston left the table. She climbed the ladder to the loft where she'd put her things. In a moment she was back with a bottle in her hand. She set the bottle on its side in the middle of the table.

Everyone leaned forward to look. Inside the bottle was a model of a three-masted ship. "This ship looks just like my father's," said Miss Winston.

Kirsten drew in a sharp breath. "It looks just like the *Eagle*, too!" she said.

Miss Winston handed Kirsten the bottle so she could get a better look. Now she saw the ship

*Kirsten drew a sharp breath.*
*"It looks just like the Eagle, too!"*

closely. "The ship we sailed on to America looked just like this one. It was called the *Eagle.* We sailed for ten weeks. There were terrible storms. Everyone was sick. Six people died on the ship, and the sailors buried them at sea." She stopped, breathless, surprised at how many words she had just blurted out in English.

Miss Winston pressed her forefinger to her lips and looked closely at Kirsten. "You remember the ship clearly, don't you?"

"Oh, yes! My friend Marta and I played on the deck," Kirsten said.

"Ah!" Miss Winston exclaimed. "You've given me an idea, Kirsten."

In school the next day, Miss Winston came to Kirsten's side right after the first song. She handed Kirsten a piece of paper. Kirsten sat up straight, her heart thudding. Miss Winston never gave out paper.

"Here is another poem for you, Kirsten. I want you to memorize it instead of the first one I gave you," Miss Winston said. "It's four lines from a long poem about a man who was a sailor all his life. When you spoke of your trip on the *Eagle,* I thought you

might like these lines. Can you read them?"

Miss Winston's writing was as perfect as the writing in a book. Kirsten held the paper in both hands and read slowly but clearly:

"Swiftly, swiftly flew the ship
Yet she sailed softly too:
Sweetly, sweetly blew the breeze—
On me alone it blew."

As she read, Kirsten could almost feel the ocean wind on her face and taste the salt spray on her lips. And she missed Marta.

"You read that well, Kirsten. Do you think you

could memorize these lines?" Miss Winston asked.

Kirsten nodded. She hoped that if she forgot any words, she could imagine the *Eagle* and the words would come back to her. "I'll try," she said.

Miss Winston bent down until her eyes were level with Kirsten's. "You will try and you will succeed. Remember that, please." Then she went to open the door of the iron stove so Amos could put in more wood to heat the classroom.

Because Kirsten and her family ate dinner at Uncle Olav's house now, it was impossible for Kirsten to meet Singing Bird at their usual time in the evening. And there was never enough time in the morning. But on Wednesday Kirsten managed to leave a tiny doll made of yarn for her friend. After school, she found a piece of blue and white beadwork in its place. She thought it would make a beautiful headband for Sari.

Beside the beads, Singing Bird had drawn a full sun in the sand. She wanted Kirsten to come early in the morning to meet her. Sadly, Kirsten

 drew a cross through the drawing to tell Singing Bird that she couldn't come. When would she be able to meet her friend again?

On Friday, Kirsten whispered to Miss Winston that she was ready to recite her verse. Her chest ached and her stomach fluttered, but she wanted to recite before she forgot the poem.

Miss Winston held up her hand and told everyone to be still. "Kirsten Larson will now recite. Please come forward, Kirsten." Miss Winston stepped back so that Kirsten could stand in front of the stove where everyone would see her.

Slowly, Kirsten walked to the center of the room. She tried to keep her chin high, just as Miss Winston did. She saw Anna's smile and Lars's grin. Then the room seemed to blur and fade, and all she heard was the thud of her heart.

"You may recite now," Miss Winston said. "With feeling, please."

*Now,* Kirsten told herself. She imagined the sails of the *Eagle* creaking overhead. She imagined sea gulls swooping and diving in the wind. She imagined Marta sitting by her side on the deck.

*She kept her eyes closed and
recited the poem without a single mistake.*

"Swiftly, swiftly flew the ship," Kirsten said. She heard her own words clearly, as though someone else had spoken them. She kept her eyes closed and recited the poem without a single mistake.

When she opened her eyes the other students were smiling at her. Miss Winston touched her shoulder. "You recited very well, Kirsten. You recited with feeling. I'm proud of you," she said.

Kirsten sat down in a daze. She had stood in front of everyone and recited her poem in English! She hadn't thought she could do it, but she had. And it hadn't been so hard, after all. The next time would be easier, she was sure of it. She'd been scared, but she had done it, and now Miss Winston was proud of her.

Anna nudged her and said, "Good for you!" Lisbeth gave her a wink that said the same thing.

"Now it's time for reading," Miss Winston said.

But Kirsten was too dizzy to read. "May I fetch the water for our drink?" she asked Miss Winston.

"Yes, Kirsten, thank you. As you walk, don't forget to take deep breaths to draw fresh air into your lungs," Miss Winston said with a smile.

Kirsten seized the bucket and her shawl.

Outside, the air was cold. A light dusting of snow lay on the ground. When she reached the stream, Kirsten found a thin coat of ice on the water.

She broke the ice easily with a stick and dipped her bucket into the stream. As she did, she heard the whistle of a meadowlark. When Kirsten looked up she saw Singing Bird standing among the ice-coated cattails on the other side of the stream.

"Hello!" Kirsten said.

"Come," Singing Bird answered.

"But I can't come with you now," Kirsten said. "I have to go back to school."

"Come," Singing Bird repeated. She crossed the stream on a fallen log.

"Maybe I can come after school," Kirsten said, though she wasn't sure how she could.

"Come *now*," Singing Bird replied. "We go today."

Kirsten grasped her friend's cold hand. "Go? You're going? But why?"

"No food," Singing Bird said. She pressed her hands to her stomach.

"Don't you have enough food?" Kirsten asked.

She remembered the terrible pains in her stomach when Papa's crops had failed in Sweden. She remembered how Peter had cried when there was no more bread to eat.

"Bad hunting," Singing Bird explained. She held up her arms as though she shot an arrow from a bow. "We go to find food."

Kirsten remembered what Lisbeth and Anna had told her. The wild animals were leaving the land because the settlers were building farms. The Indians didn't have enough to eat. They were leaving to find more food.

"Where will you go?" Kirsten asked. When Papa couldn't grow enough food in Sweden, they had come here to America. Where could the Indians go to find better hunting?

Singing Bird pointed west. "We go there. For buffalo. For deer." Then she stroked the blond braids which looped over Kirsten's ears. "You come too," Singing Bird said.

Kirsten looked at the snow-covered hill where a hawk circled in the sky. Then she looked at her friend's dark face, so close to her own.

113

"Come, sister," Singing Bird said. She took Kirsten's hand.

Kirsten remembered the warm tepee where Singing Bird lived. She imagined herself sleeping by Singing Bird's side under the buffalo hides. If she lived with Singing Bird she would be free to roam the woods all day. Brave Elk would be good to her. He was the chief, and Kirsten would be his yellow-haired daughter. She and Singing Bird would always be together.

But how could Kirsten leave her own parents, her brothers, her cousins? How could she leave the cabin under the pines? If she didn't come back home, Mama and Papa would be wild with worry. They would think she was lost. They might even think she'd been killed. And they would never give her permission to go with Singing Bird.

"No. I *can't* come with you," Kirsten said. "I want to come, but this is my home. I can't leave my home," Kirsten said.

Singing Bird looked down sadly. She reached into the pouch she wore around her waist and took out her bone needle. She gave it to Kirsten.

Kirsten closed her hand around the bone needle. "Will you come back, Singing Bird?"

Singing Bird shook her head. "If deer come back," she said.

"Oh, please, do come back!" Kirsten said. "I'll be here. Right here. You can find me easily. Whistle for me by the stream."

"If deer come back," Singing Bird repeated. She touched Kirsten's braid one last time. Then she ran back to the fallen log and crossed the stream. She waved from the edge of the pine forest before she disappeared into the snow-covered trees.

Kirsten watched her friend go. She imagined
Singing Bird's tribe hungry, wandering, looking for

food. Where would they go? How far
would they have to travel before they
could set up their village again? Now
Kirsten understood that if the settlers
made a home here, the Indians would
have to find a new home.

She filled her water bucket and trudged slowly
back to the school. She pushed open the door to the
warm room. Miss Winston looked up from her place
by the stove. "You've been gone a long time, Kirsten.
I thought you'd found that ship in your poem and
sailed back to Sweden!"

"No, ma'am," Kirsten said softly. She knew it
was a joke, but she was too sad to smile. She slipped
her hand into her pocket and touched the bone
needle. How she would miss Singing Bird!

Miss Winston smiled, though. "I left something
for you. It's in your reader," she said.

Kirsten looked around the cozy room crowded
with busy children. She wasn't sure when this place
had become her own, but she belonged here now.
Her reader lay on the bench waiting for her.

"Will you help me again?" she asked Anna.

"Yes!" Anna said gladly, as she always did, and made room on the bench. Kirsten sat down and opened her book.

FOR MY MOTHER,
NADINA FOWLER

# 1854
# KIRSTEN'S
# SURPRISE
## *A Christmas Story*

# PESTERING

The first year that Kirsten and her family lived in the little log cabin on Uncle Olav's farm in Minnesota, the autumn weather lasted into December. Although the stream froze and they had to melt ice for water, there was only a little snow. Papa often stroked his beard and pointed to the geese flying south. "A very hard winter's on the way," he said. "It will be much colder here than in Sweden. We have to get ready for the deep snows." But Kirsten thought the traces of snow on the pines looked like the sugar Mama sprinkled on gingersnaps—light and sweet. It was hard to believe winter was coming.

One day when Kirsten came into the cabin after

school, she smelled cinnamon. "Something smells delicious," she said. "What are you making, Mama?"

Mama had her sleeves rolled up and her apron on. "It's time to bake Christmas bread," she answered. "Come help me."

Kirsten washed her hands and tied one of Mama's long aprons over her school dress. "Don't forget to cover your hands with flour so the dough won't stick," Mama said. She took several loaves of risen bread dough from the cupboard and set them on the pine table in front of Kirsten.

Kirsten pushed her fingers into the dough and punched it down. When the air was out of the dough, she shaped it into round loaves to rise a second time. The smells of yeast and spices made her mouth water.

"Will Christmas in America be just like it was in Sweden?" Kirsten asked Mama.

Mama wiped her hands on her apron. "I don't know, Kirsten. Some things here are different. And you know we don't have money for extra treats. But we'll do the best we can." Mama must have seen that Kirsten was disappointed, for she added,

*"Will Christmas in America be just
like it was in Sweden?" Kirsten asked.*

"Here, take a piece of dough and make a loaf of bread for your doll."

As Kirsten rolled the piece of dough between her palms, she glanced at Little Sari. Little Sari lay on Kirsten's trundle bed. She wasn't a real doll at all. She was only a worn stocking stuffed with milk-weed floss. Kirsten had made her because she missed her real Sari so much. Real Sari, with her pretty face and her blue dress, was still far away in Riverton. Kirsten had to leave her there last summer, when all the money Papa had saved for their trip to America was gone. He couldn't hire a wagon to carry their trunks, so they'd left most of their things in a warehouse and walked the last twenty miles to Uncle Olav's farm.

"I wish I had my real Sari," Kirsten said. She set the little doll loaf of bread on the wooden tray with the big loaves Mama had shaped.

"I know you miss your doll," Mama said. "But work comes before play. We needed both your hands to carry tools and blankets that day." Mama's voice softened. "And you'll see Sari again soon. Mr. Berkhoff sent word that the trunks have been shipped as far as his store in Maryville. When Papa has time, he can take the wagon and get them."

"Oh, could he go today?" Kirsten asked happily.

"Maryville is ten miles away, Kirsten," Mama said. "It will take Papa half a day to get there and back with the wagon. It's too late to go today."

"Will he go tomorrow?"

"No, Kirsten," Mama said. "He won't have time tomorrow."

"Couldn't we just ask him?" Kirsten said.

"It would only make him cross to ask," Mama said. "Papa is too busy now."

"When *will* Papa have time?" Kirsten knew she was pestering Mama, but she wanted the trunks and Sari so badly that she couldn't help herself.

Mama leaned across the table to brush flour off Kirsten's nose. "You know Papa and Uncle Olav have to get the farm ready for winter. That comes first. Be patient a little while longer, Kirsten."

"Well, why don't you and I take the wagon and get the trunks? You know how to drive the horse and wagon, Mama!"

Now Mama smiled. "You're full of ideas today!

But there's school for you tomorrow, and we aren't strong enough to lift those big trunks. We can get along with what we have until Papa has his work done."

"But don't you want the shawl Mormor made for you, and your candlesticks?" Kirsten asked. She looked around the bare little cabin. "We all need the heavy quilts and our warm clothes for winter. And Papa needs his hand tools, and I need Sari. Or at least I miss her. Don't you miss your things, too?"

Mama patted the last loaf of bread and set it on the tray. "People are more important than things, Kirsten."

Kirsten traced a heart shape in the flour on the table. "You always say that, Mama. But things help me remember people, too. When I wear my sweater from Mormor, I can picture her knitting it for me. If I could see the Christmas cloths you both wove for the rafters, I'd feel like she was here with us."

Mama had the dough tray halfway into the cupboard, but now she stopped and looked closely at Kirsten. Even in the dim cabin Mama's eyes were as blue as the cloudless sky. "You're a

126

wise girl, Kirsten. Our things can have special meanings for us. They help us remember. I feel just as you do."

"You do?" Kirsten asked.

Mama nodded. "I often think of the day we finished packing the painted trunk to bring to America. Do you remember that day?"

"I remember it was spring and there were buds on the maple tree. Mormor and your friend Mrs. Hanson came early in the morning and stayed all day to help us," Kirsten said.

"We were used to working together," Mama said softly. "How carefully Mormor folded our sweaters. And Mrs. Hanson brought dried lavender to put in with our linens so they would smell sweet when we unpacked them here." Mama gazed at the window as though she could see Kirsten's grandmother and Mrs. Hanson right now.

"I remember how you all laughed when Peter begged to put his sled into the trunk," Kirsten said.

"And how we all cried when we said good-bye," Mama whispered. "We knew we would never see each other again."

Kirsten was surprised to see tears in Mama's

blue eyes. She didn't know that Mama could get homesick, too.

"Mama, are you all right?" Kirsten asked.

Abruptly, Mama turned and shoved the bread tray into the cupboard. "Of course I'm all right." She poured coffee into the coffee pail and held it out to Kirsten. "Now take this hot coffee out to the barn for Papa. He forgets to rest and warm himself unless we remind him. Let's get on with our work, Kirsten."

Papa stood in the back of the wagon to fork hay into the barn. His cheeks were red from work and from cold. He climbed down and took the coffee pail from Kirsten. "Just what I need," he said as he sipped the steaming coffee. Bits of hay stuck to his work jacket and his beard.

Kirsten leaned against the wagon wheel. "Papa, could you go to town tomorrow and get the trunks? Mama and I need some things from the painted trunk especially."

Papa glanced at Kirsten over the rim of the pail as he sipped. "When all our work is done here I'll go for the trunks," he said. "First things first."

Kirsten looked around at the wide fields. The farm was large, and she could see that there was still much to be done. "When will all the work be finished?" she asked.

"It *must* be done before the heavy snows come or we won't get through the winter. Now don't pester me, Kirsten," he said gruffly. But when he handed her back the empty coffee pail he patted her shoulder. "I'll get the trunks as soon as I have time."

But Papa didn't have time. The hogs had to be butchered and the meat smoked. Papa and Uncle Olav spent a whole week repairing fences. They put new runners on the sleigh and new shoes on the horse. In the evenings they mended harness leather and stuffed extra clay between the logs in the cabin walls to make the cabin warmer. They put up a fence to keep snowdrifts off the path to the barn. When the heavy snows came it would be too late to do these important things.

Kirsten knew that when the heavy snows came it would be too late to get the trunks, too. The drifts would block the road into Maryville, and the snow wouldn't melt until spring. She couldn't wait until spring to have Sari back! The more Kirsten thought about the trunks, the more reasons she found for wanting them. Surely Lars wanted his skates, and Peter wanted his clay whistle. And she thought that unpacking the painted trunk would be like a visit home to Sweden for Mama. Every night when she said her prayers she prayed that Papa would get the trunks soon.

# A CROWN
# FOR A QUEEN

Kirsten sat with Lisbeth and Anna in
a cozy corner of the barn. These days it
was much too cold to play in their fort
under the cherry tree, so they brought their dolls
inside and scooped out rooms for them in the sweet-
smelling hay. The barn cats prowled around,
switching their tails. But they were too wild to be
petted or put into doll dresses.

Kirsten was trying to make a dress for Little
Sari. She wrapped Little Sari in one of Papa's white
handkerchiefs and tied a piece of red yarn around
it for a sash. Then she pretended to walk Little Sari
across the hay to Anna. "Do you think Little Sari
looks like Saint Lucia?" she asked Anna.

Anna looked up in surprise. "Who?"

"Saint Lucia. Don't you know Saint Lucia?" Kirsten asked, puzzled.

Anna shook her head. "Is she someone you knew in Sweden?"

Now Kirsten was really startled. "No, Anna. We celebrated Saint Lucia's Day in Sweden. It was the very best part of Christmas."

"I don't remember Sweden," Lisbeth said. "I was just a baby when Mama left. We just celebrate Christmas Day."

Kirsten's spirits fell. She'd hoped this first Christmas in America would be just like Christmas in Sweden. How could it, if they didn't have Saint Lucia's Day? She thought Mama would be disappointed, too. It was her favorite celebration.

"Tell us about Saint Lucia's Day," Anna said. She sat her doll on her lap as though the doll listened, too.

"In Sweden, Saint Lucia's Day begins the Christmas season," Kirsten explained. "It's the darkest day of the whole year. It's so dark that there's only daylight for a few hours. But no one minds the dark, because Saint Lucia's Day is such fun."

*"Tell us about Saint Lucia's Day,"*
*Anna said.*

Lisbeth was braiding a straw belt for her doll. "What do you do?"

"In each family, one girl gets to be the Lucia queen. She dresses up in a long white dress and a red sash, and she wears a crown of green leaves and lighted candles. She gets up very, very early in the morning, while it's still pitch black and everyone is asleep. She lights the candles in her crown, and she goes from room to room in the dark house, carrying a tray. First she goes to her parents' room. Even though they've helped her get ready, they can hardly believe their eyes when they see her, she looks so beautiful in her costume. Then she wakes all the rest of the family and invites them to share Lucia buns and coffee. That breakfast is the first party of the holiday season," Kirsten explained.

Anna's gray eyes grew wider and she hugged herself. "Oh, a white dress and a crown! It sounds beautiful. I wish *we* had Saint Lucia's Day."

That gave Kirsten an idea. She motioned for her cousins to draw closer together. "Why don't we make a Saint Lucia's celebration? Just the three of us!

We won't tell our parents or the boys. We'll get everything ready and surprise them. Wouldn't that be fun?"

Anna's round face glowed with excitement. "We'll keep it a secret! Oh, I love secrets!"

But Lisbeth cocked her head and frowned. "It would be exciting, all right. But how could we get all the special things we'd need?"

"That won't be hard," Kirsten insisted. "Mama always has coffee, and we can slice a loaf of our Christmas bread and pretend it's Lucia buns. That takes care of the tray."

"How about the crown?" Lisbeth asked.

"I think we could make one from a wild grapevine and wintergreen leaves. It shouldn't be too hard to do." As Kirsten planned, she grew more and more excited.

Now Anna was too eager to sit still. She hopped to her feet and waved her arms, and the cats scattered and hissed. "You can be Saint Lucia, Kirsten, because you know how," Anna cried.

"But where will we get a white dress and red sash?" asked Lisbeth.

"I have a white dress!" Kirsten answered.

"Well, it's really a white nightdress, but it's just what we need. I wore it last year for Saint Lucia's Day. It's in our trunk."

Now the three girls looked at each other in silence. Then they each let out a sigh. "But your trunks aren't *here*," Lisbeth said.

"When is Saint Lucia's Day?" Anna asked.

"It's December thirteenth," Kirsten said. Quickly she counted on her fingers. "That's five whole days from now."

Lisbeth shrugged sadly. "Then it's no use planning. If your father doesn't get that trunk, there's no white dress and sash."

Anna let herself tumble backward into the hay. When she got up, hay was stuck in her braids. "It was a grand idea. But we don't have candles for the crown, either. Mama would surely miss them if we took them without asking her."

But now Kirsten was determined to make a Saint Lucia celebration. She *had* to think of something. Of course! They could ask Miss Winston!

Kirsten got to her knees and grabbed Anna's ankle to get her attention. "We could ask Miss

Winston to get us some candles and to help us."
Miss Winston was the teacher at Powderkeg School.
She'd been living at Uncle Olav's house for several
weeks and would stay there all winter, until she
moved in with another family.

Anna grinned. "Oh, I know Miss Winston would
like a party. She's been telling us about the Christmas
parties they had back East. It makes her sad to think
she'll miss them. And she has extra candles in her
trunk!"

"That still leaves the dress," Lisbeth said slowly.
"I don't know . . ."

"Lisbeth, Papa practically promised me that he'd
get the trunks soon," Kirsten said. "We'll make all
the things we need, and we'll practice. When he gets
the trunks, we'll be ready!"

Lisbeth looked relieved. "We should start getting
everything ready now. We'll have to practice up in
our room so the boys won't know what we're doing."

"And we'll have to hide the crown under the
bed, won't we?" Anna cried. "Or under Miss
Winston's bed. They'd never look there!"

Suddenly Lisbeth held her finger to her lips.
"Shhhhh!"

Kirsten listened. She heard the cows mooing and Papa's deep voice as he brought them in to be milked. "It's Papa," she whispered.

"Go right now and ask him to get the trunks," Lisbeth said. "Tell him it's important!"

Kirsten took a deep breath. She knew how Papa hated to be pestered. But she had to ask him about the trunks one more time. She climbed out of the hay and went over to Papa, who sat on a small stool milking a brown cow. He leaned his forehead against the cow's side. Steam rose from the pail of warm milk.

"Papa, I've been thinking about our trunks again. Can't you *please* get them soon?" Kirsten said.

Papa's breath was a white cloud at his lips. He raised his eyebrows. "Just why are the trunks so important, Kirsten?"

Kirsten stubbed her boot against the empty bucket. "I remembered our candlesticks are in the painted trunk. Mama will want the candlesticks for Christmas."

"We all want things we can't have. I've heard enough about that trunk," Papa said. He squirted a stream of milk into the mouth of the gray cat by Kirsten's feet.

"*Please*, Papa."

Now Papa scowled. "Don't ask me again or I'll be angry!"

Kirsten walked slowly to the stall where Blackie, Uncle Olav's horse, munched hay. She patted his coat, which was thickened against the cold. "What can I do now?" she murmured to Blackie. "Every-thing depends on that trunk." Blackie snuffled and pushed his soft nose against her hand as though he sensed she needed comfort.

On the way home from school the next day, Kirsten cut a length of grapevine and Lisbeth picked wintergreen. They took them to Anna and Lisbeth's sleeping loft to work on the Saint Lucia crown.

Miss Winston was there. She sat on her bed to grade arithmetic tests. "Of course you may use some of my candles," she said when they asked her for them. She took three new candles from the trunk at the foot of her bed and cut them in two to make them the right length. "I'll hide the crown in my trunk, if you like," Miss Winston added. "I like surprises, too."

So that part was easy. But making the crown was harder. The first crown Lisbeth braided was too small. "It looks like a bird's nest," Anna said when she saw it perched on top of Kirsten's head.

The second crown Lisbeth made was much too large. It slipped right down over Kirsten's head and lay around her neck. "And that one looks like Blackie's harness," Anna told her.

"Measure Kirsten's head first," Miss Winston suggested. She gave Lisbeth a piece of string.

Lisbeth tied the string around Kirsten's head. Then she braided the grapevine exactly the size of the circle of string. This time the crown fit perfectly. Lisbeth stuck sprigs of wintergreen into the braided vine and Miss Winston set the candles in securely.

Then they decided how the tray would be laid out. "We'll have coffee and Christmas bread, and a candle in the center. All the lights will be out except for the candles," Kirsten said. "Saint Lucia comes into a dark room with her crown glowing!"

Anna put the crown on her own head and pretended to carry a tray. She walked slowly around the room. "What does Saint Lucia say now?" she asked.

"Say, 'Saint Lucia invites you to breakfast,'" Kirsten told her.

Anna cried, "Oh, this is fun!"

Lisbeth came to sit on the bed beside Kirsten. She took Kirsten's hand. "This *is* a good plan, really it is. If your trunk doesn't come in time for Saint Lucia's Day, we can have the celebration next year. Don't worry, Kirsten," Lisbeth said.

But Kirsten couldn't help but worry. She had butterflies in her stomach. She'd gotten everyone's hopes up, especially her own. And she was afraid to ask Papa about the trunk again. She would just have to wait and see what happened. There was nothing else she could do now.

THREE

—

# TO TOWN
## AT LAST

On Tuesday, Kirsten woke to the sound of voices. Except for the fire in the stove, the cabin was so dark and cold that she could see her breath. From her bed, she saw that thick ice covered the little window. Peter and Lars still slept, their heads almost hidden under their covers. But Mama and Papa were up. They sat at the pine table, talking softly. Kirsten stayed under her quilt and listened.

"We finished putting up the snow fences yesterday," Papa said. "I think we were just in time. It looks like we'll have another heavy snow soon. But I could drive into town today. Olav won't need the horse. What do you think?"

"If it's safe to go, you should try. One more hard snow and the roads will be blocked until spring," Mama said.

"Will you pack me a lunch, then? I'll leave as soon as the milking is done and be back with the trunks before suppertime," Papa said.

The trunks! Now Kirsten was wide awake, her heart pounding. Tomorrow was Saint Lucia's Day! They would get the trunks just in time!

She was out of her bed with a leap. She ran across the rough boards of the cabin floor and threw her arms around Mama's neck. "Oh, Mama, please may I go along in the wagon to get our trunks? It doesn't matter if I miss one day of school!"

Papa was already pulling on his heavy boots. "There's too much snow for the wagon. I'm going to hitch Blackie to the sleigh, and there's not much room in that small sleigh, Kirsten."

"But *I* don't take up much room!" Kirsten cried.

"It's a long drive. You'll get cold. Go to school with your brothers," Papa said.

"But I want to go with you more than anything in the world, Papa!"

"Do you want to come with me that much?"

Papa asked. "What will you do?"

"I can help you, I'm sure of it. I can keep you company so you won't get lonely," Kirsten said. "Please say yes!"

She thought Papa might scowl because he didn't like to be urged to change his mind. But instead he laughed. "You have a strong will, Kirsten! Just like your mama! You may come with me. Eat your breakfast and dress in your warmest clothes, then bring in a bucket of snow so Mama will have water today. I'll hitch up the sleigh and we'll be on our way. Hurry, now."

Kirsten hurried. She put on two pairs of wool stockings, all of her quilted petticoats, her heaviest sweater, and a shawl. As she ate her pancakes, she watched Mama pack a lunch in the hamper and heat stones in the oven. The warm stones would keep Kirsten's and Papa's feet cozy in the sleigh.

The first rays of light came through the clouds as Papa brought the sleigh from the barn. Kirsten climbed into the sleigh beside Papa, and Mama handed her the food hamper. "Here's your lunch. And I put in a loaf of Christmas bread for you to give Mr. Berkhoff at the store. We might not see him again until spring. Tell him we wish him a happy Christmas."

Mama stood by the gate and waved as the sleigh pulled away down the road. "Take care!" she called after them.

Blackie whinnied and stamped. The harness bells around his neck jingled merrily. Kirsten laughed with pleasure when she heard the bells. She remembered the wonderful holidays in Sweden, the sleigh rides they'd taken to church and to the homes of their friends.

Snow was falling as Kirsten and Papa left the farm. The snowflakes settled on Blackie's back like moths and caught in Kirsten's eyelashes. Papa turned the horse east toward the small town of Maryville. Now the wind was at their backs. Under a fur blanket, Kirsten was snug by Papa's side.

Papa's wide-brimmed hat was pulled low. He wore his sheepskin mittens with high tops that came up over his jacket cuffs, and a red scarf Mama had knitted for him. As they slid along, he began to sing a Christmas carol. His deep voice seemed to fill up his whole chest and to push ahead of them through

the softly falling snow.

Kirsten sang, too. She was happy. In no time they'd pick up their trunks and be back at the farm. Then, tomorrow morning before dawn, she and Lisbeth and Anna would surprise everyone with the Saint Lucia celebration. Their plans were turning out perfectly after all.

By the time they reached Maryville it was snowing harder. The soft snow made caps on the

146

tops of the fenceposts and piled up on the shingled rooftops. Kirsten and Papa drove past houses, the church, and the sawmill, then stopped in front of Berkhoff's General Store. While Papa unhitched Blackie from the sleigh, Kirsten watched the men and women in the street. She was glad to smell woodsmoke in the air and to hear people greeting one another. Maryville was only a little town, but it had a happy bustle.

Inside the store, the delicious scents of spices, new cloth, oiled leather, and sausages reached Kirsten's nose all at once. Mr. Berkhoff stood behind the scales, weighing sugar. When he saw Kirsten and Papa, he wiped his hands on his white apron and came around the counter to shake Papa's hand. He gave Kirsten a piece of hard sugar candy from one of the glass jars. "It's not Christmas yet, but have a little treat," he said.

Kirsten handed him the loaf of Christmas bread Mama had sent. "Mama sends you a merry Christmas greeting," she said. "And thank you for the candy."

Mr. Berkhoff raised his white eyebrows.

147

"Kirsten Larson, the last time you were in my store
you spoke to me in Swedish!"

Kirsten felt herself blush. "I'm learning English."

"So you are! And you speak it very well, too,"
Mr. Berkhoff said. "Thank your mother for the
bread."

"We're here to pick up our trunks," Papa said.

"Come with me," Mr. Berkhoff said. He took
them to a big storage room at the back of the store.
Wooden boxes and barrels were piled clear up to
the ceiling. Mr. Berkhoff pushed aside some crates
to let Kirsten and Papa through. There, by the back

door, they saw the two big trunks
with "Anders Larson" painted on
their sides.

Papa slapped the trunks with
his open hand the way he slapped
the cows. "Well, Kirsten, here are our things at last!"

Kirsten leaned against the painted trunk. She
traced the flower paintings with her fingertip. Sari
was in this trunk—right there under the lid. The
white nightdress and red sash she needed for Saint
Lucia's Day would be near all of Mama's lovely
weavings. And at the bottom of the trunk there
were heavy woolen sweaters, caps, mittens, and the
shiny brass candlesticks. Oh, everything was in this
trunk! It seemed like an old dear friend Kirsten had
met again after a long time. She pressed her cheek
against the rounded top.

"Papa, let's open the trunk now!" she said.
"I want to hold Sari on the sleigh ride home."

Papa and Mr. Berkhoff pushed the trunks out
the back door onto the loading platform. "We'll open
the trunks when we get them home," Papa said.
"We've got to go right now. It's snowing harder, and
we have a long drive back home."

Mr. Berkhoff squinted up into the snow. "Maybe you folks should stay here until the snow stops, Mr. Larson."

"Thank you," Papa said, "but I think we'll leave now before this snow gets heavier."

"Don't get lost," Mr. Berkhoff warned. "This looks like it will be a storm." He lifted Kirsten into the sleigh beside Papa.

"Merry Christmas!" Kirsten called back to Mr. Berkhoff as Papa drove the sleigh away from the store.

Mr. Berkhoff's answering call was muffled by the thud of Blackie's steps in the snow. "Merry Christmas to you, too!"

C H A P T E R
F O U R

—

# BRAVING THE
# BLIZZARD

As they left Maryville in the loaded
sleigh, the snow seemed to fall harder
every minute. It stung Kirsten's cheeks
until she pulled her shawl up over her nose. Papa
urged Blackie faster, but now the horse had the extra
weight of the trunks to pull and the sleigh didn't
skim along as it had done before. "Look at that sky!"
Papa said. "The weather changed while we waited
in the store."

When the road turned west toward the farm,
Kirsten saw that the sleigh tracks they'd made earlier
were filling with snow. The strong wind drove the
snow directly into their faces. There was no way to
hide from it.

"Pull the blanket over your head," Papa told Kirsten.

She curled up next to Papa's side and buried her face under his arm. She could hear the thump of Papa's heart and the muffled jingle of the sleigh bells as Blackie trotted along.

The next time Kirsten peeked over the edge of the blanket all she could see was white. Snow swirled up from the fields like spray blown from the tops of waves. Drifts shifted and moved as Blackie stepped along. Papa's beard was filled with snow, his mustache was white with it. His eyes were blue slits under his snow-caked eyebrows.

"Where's the road, Papa?" Kirsten asked.

"I can't see it. We're following the fenceposts. Blackie can find his way, though. He's a smart horse," Papa said.

"Do you think we should go back to Maryville?"

"We've already come a long way. I think there's a better chance the horse knows his way to the farm. If we just keep heading west we'll be all right." But Papa frowned into the fiercely blowing snow.

Kirsten was worried, too. She'd heard stories about settlers who lost their way in blizzards and walked in circles until they fell down. She'd heard about a boy who froze to death when he got lost between his barn and his house. A snowstorm on the plains was as dangerous as a storm on the ocean.

Blackie's harness bells sounded faint and lost. His ears were down, his head low. Papa urged him to keep going, but the horse often stumbled in the moving drifts. Kirsten's feet were so cold she could barely move her toes. Under her feet, she felt the stones Mama had heated that morning. The warmth had long since gone out of them.

"Toss the stones out of the sleigh," Papa told her. "We should make this load lighter. The trunks are heavier than I remembered."

"But we won't leave our trunks in the snow, will we?" Kirsten asked.

Papa patted her knee. "No, we won't leave our trunks. This snow will let up soon, you'll see." He slapped the reins against Blackie's back, which was thickly covered with snow.

Then there were no more fenceposts to follow.

153

*Kirsten had heard stories about settlers
who lost their way in blizzards.*

They drove along beside a dim shadow that
Kirsten knew was the edge of the forest. But
Blackie walked more and more slowly.
Often Papa had to flick the whip across
his back to keep him moving.

"He wants to turn his back to the wind," Papa
said. "But we have to go straight into the wind if
we're going to get back to the farm."

"Keep going, Blackie!" Kirsten shouted. Her
words seemed to disappear into the snow and wind.

All at once Blackie stopped. He wouldn't move.
"Yo!" Papa yelled. "Get up there!"

It was no use. The horse wouldn't take a single
step.

"What's wrong with him?" Kirsten asked.

"He loses his footing in the snow, and that
frightens him," Papa said. "I'll have to lead him to
keep him moving."

Papa handed Kirsten the reins, wrapped the
blanket tightly around her waist, and climbed down
from the sleigh. He stepped through snowdrifts to
Blackie's head and took hold of his bridle. "Come
on, Blackie! Come along, now!" Papa made his
voice both gruff and soothing. The horse took one

step, stopped, then took another step. The bells jingled again.

Kirsten realized she'd been holding her breath. She let it out with a sigh. Blackie trusted Papa. Now they'd keep going toward home.

They went slowly, step by difficult step. Papa climbed through knee-high drifts. Even though he was only a few feet in front of her, Kirsten could hardly see him. He was completely covered with snow. Papa pulled Blackie's bridle, and Kirsten slapped Blackie's flanks with the reins.

The snow and cold made Kirsten light-headed. Sometimes it seemed the sleigh wasn't moving at all. Only the snow seemed to move, like water running in a stream.

Then Papa stumbled. He went down on his knees and cried out. Kirsten had never heard Papa cry out in pain before, and the sound was colder than the wind.

"Papa!" she shouted. "Papa, are you all right?"

She jumped out of the sleigh. The snow came up to her hips, but Kirsten pushed through it to Papa's side.

Papa tried to stand, but again he went down in the snow.

"What's the matter, Papa?"

"My knee. I twisted my knee. I can't put my weight on it," he said. His face was very pale, his lips white. There was ice in his mustache.

"What can I do?" Kirsten begged him.

"Nothing, Kirsten. It's up to Blackie now," Papa answered. "We can't stop here. We have to reach shelter." He dragged himself back to the sleigh, breathing hard. Kirsten wondered how he would ever get back onto the high front seat.

At last Papa managed to crawl up. Then he reached down to help Kirsten up beside him. But when he snapped the whip over Blackie's back, the horse wouldn't budge.

"It's no good," Papa said. "With no one to lead him, he'll stay right here."

Kirsten grabbed Papa's hand. "But *I* can lead Blackie!" she said. "You stay in the sleigh, and I'll walk beside him."

"Do you think you can walk through this deep snow?"

"I'll try, Papa!"

Papa brushed the snow off Kirsten's shoulders and tied her shawl more tightly over her nose and mouth. Then he pulled off his sheepskin mittens and put them on her hands. Inside Papa's mittens the fleece was warm and dry. Kirsten's cold hands felt like rabbits creeping into a snug home.

"You're a good girl, Kirsten," Papa said. "You have heart."

Papa had told Mama she had heart when she agreed to come here to America. He told Mama she had heart when she was sick on the ship but didn't lose hope. Kirsten wanted to be as brave as Mama. She pulled herself along Blackie's side. She shook the harness and made the bells sound. "Yo!" she cried in the biggest voice she could manage. "Yo, Blackie! Come along!" To her surprise, the horse's head came up and he followed her.

But the going was hard. Kirsten's feet slipped. The drifts were up to her knees, and now her feet were so numb she couldn't even wiggle her toes. Like the horse, she bent her head into the wind and concentrated on just one step, then the next, then the next.

Snow caked on her lips. *Keep going,* she told herself. *Have heart, Kirsten.* But she didn't know where she was going. The whole world was a white blowing snowdrift. And it would soon be dark. Then how would they ever, ever find the way home?

Kirsten tried to imagine their home, the little snug cabin somewhere in this storm. It would be warm there. She imagined Mama making soup for supper. She imagined Lisbeth and Anna waiting to make the Saint Lucia's Day surprise.

*Keep going,* Kirsten told herself. She tried to sing a Christmas carol to keep her spirits up. But her lips were so cold she could barely move them. Instead, she began to count the way Miss Winston drilled numbers in school. *One, two, three, four*—that was four steps closer to home. *Five, six, seven, eight*—eight steps closer to home. Kirsten was glad she'd learned her numbers. Maybe the numbers would keep her moving. *Nine, ten, eleven*—she bumped into something. She fell against Blackie's side and looked around. They weren't in the fields near the forest anymore. They were near some rocks.

"We've come the wrong way," Papa called. "The horse has taken us into a valley by the stream. He's lost."

Kirsten shielded her eyes from the snow to look. She knew where they were! Blackie hadn't come the wrong way at all! These were the cliffs she'd gone to with Singing Bird, her Indian friend. There was the forked birch tree, bent over by the wind. She knew that tree! She'd passed it on her way to the cave where she and Singing Bird had sometimes played.

Kirsten struggled back to Papa. She reached

up and grabbed his hand. "I know where we are, Papa!"

"How can you know where we are, Kirsten? The horse has lost his way."

"I've been here!" Kirsten cried.

"You've been here? Where are we?" Papa asked.

"We're beside a cliff. There's a tiny cave nearby." Kirsten pointed.

Papa looked up at the cliff. "How far to the cave?"

"It's only a little way. And there's dry wood inside. We can stay there until the storm is over," Kirsten said.

Papa tried to stand, but his leg gave out and he sat down again. "Can you take care of Blackie?" he asked.

"Yes, I'm sure I can."

"Then unharness him from the sleigh and lead him to that clump of birch trees. He'll rest there and be glad of it." Groaning, Papa crawled down from the sleigh. He sat on the snow and pushed himself backwards, inching up the slope toward the opening of the cave.

As Papa climbed, Kirsten took Blackie's harness off. It was hard to do in Papa's big mittens, so she pulled one off and held it in her teeth while she worked at the buckle. Blackie followed her a few yards to the shelter of the clump of trees. As she tied his reins to the birch tree, he whinnied.

Kirsten brushed the snow from his forelock and his face. "Good old Blackie! You have heart, do you know that? You're a very brave horse!" Then she followed Papa up the path to the cave.

Inside, the cave was dry and not very deep. Near the back was a pile of dry sticks and grass, and the black traces of campfires the Indians had made. Singing Bird had said that they sometimes stayed here when they were hunting.

Papa twisted a handful of dry grass, then laid dry sticks over it. He chipped at a piece of stone with his flint until he got sparks. A tiny flame began in the dry grass. Papa blew gently and the sticks caught fire. Kirsten brought a larger branch and laid it by the little fire.

"First we must warm up your feet, Kirsten. Take

*"When did you come to this cave?"*
*Papa asked.*

off your boots," Papa said. He leaned against the dry wall of the cave.

Kirsten spread the blanket next to Papa, sat down, and loosened her bootlaces. When she got her boots off, Papa began to rub her feet gently with his warm hands. Soon her toes started to tingle. She knew it was a good sign that they hurt—they weren't frozen.

Papa took off his own boots now and put a thick log on the fire. "When did you come to this cave?" he asked her.

Because Kirsten didn't want to tell him about Singing Bird and the Indians, she said, "I was exploring along the stream, and I found it."

"Did you have permission to be so far from the farm?" Papa asked sternly.

Kirsten shook her head. "No, Papa. I wandered farther than I thought."

The ice was melting from Papa's beard, and she saw that he smiled at her. "I'm glad that you're a little explorer, Kirsten. I'm glad you found this cave. Do you think you can find your way back to the farm from here?"

"I think so, Papa."

"Then lie back and rest," Papa said. "There's nothing we can do until it stops snowing, and you must be very, very tired."

Now that they were resting, Kirsten realized she was hungry. She was too exhausted to climb down the path and get what was left of their lunch from the sleigh. But in her pocket she found the piece of sugar candy Mr. Berkhoff had given her at the general store. The candy was shaped like a Christmas bell. She put it in her mouth and lay down beside Papa. The last thing she knew before she fell into a deep sleep was the taste of cinnamon and sugar on her tongue.

165

# CHAPTER
## FIVE

# SILENT NIGHT, LUCIA LIGHT

When Kirsten woke, Papa was brushing dirt on the fire to put it out. Outside, it was very dark. The night sky was clear, but there was no moon. "The storm's gone past," Papa said. "Now we can make our way home if you can lead Blackie. I still can't stand on my leg."

Kirsten rubbed her eyes and sat up. "I can lead him," she said. She rolled up the blanket, and Papa helped her into her boots, which he'd warmed by the fire. While Papa crawled slowly down the path, she untied Blackie and hitched him to the sleigh.

The fresh snow gleamed in the starlight. *It must be very late if the moon has gone down,* Kirsten thought. She imagined Mama peering out of the cabin window, looking for them. Mama would be worried.

As Kirsten led Blackie beside the stream, she watched for familiar landmarks. From time to time she looked back at Papa in the sleigh and at the painted trunk under its roof of snow. The sleigh bells jingled crisply in the still night.

At last Kirsten recognized a big oak tree and the curve in the stream where she'd often met Singing Bird. But the woods looked different in the deep snow. Was this the place where they should turn to find the farm? She hesitated. Blackie nudged her with his nose. Yes, this must be the way.

Before Kirsten saw the cabin and Uncle Olav's house, she smelled woodsmoke. Then they came around a turn and she saw that candles lit up all the windows of Uncle Olav's house. Everyone was waiting there. They had stayed up all night to look for her and Papa.

Kirsten led Blackie right up to Uncle Olav's door. As they approached, Papa shouted, "We're here! We're safe!"

Faces appeared at all the windows. The door

swung wide, and Mama ran out. "Here you are at last. We were so worried," she said as she hugged Kirsten. "But you're hurt!" she added when she saw Papa. She climbed into the sleigh to hug him, too.

Everyone crowded around the sleigh, asking questions. Uncle Olav helped Papa down from the sleigh, and Aunt Inger said, "I'll heat some soup to warm your chilly bones." Lisbeth, Anna, and Miss Winston all hugged Kirsten, and even Lars squeezed her shoulder before he went to untie the trunks. Peter was jumping up and down in front of the stove. "We stayed up all night to watch for you! Even Miss Winston stayed up all night," he said.

For a moment, Kirsten stood in the doorway to the kitchen and just stared. It seemed to her that she and Papa had been gone for days instead of hours. And now the world seemed turned upside down. It was the middle of the night, but in the kitchen, where all the lamps were lit, it was as bright as day. Aunt Inger bustled about heating the potato soup, but everyone was wearing nightclothes. Kirsten smiled to see Uncle Olav with his nightshirt tucked into his trousers and his sleeping cap still on his head. She smiled to see Anna in her nightgown and Mama's sweater, which trailed down to the floor. Even Miss Winston's hair was unbraided, although she had gotten dressed.

At last Kirsten sat near the warm stove with a bowl of hot soup in front of her. Mama hugged her once more, so hard she was nearly lifted from her chair. "Oh, I knew you shouldn't have gone with Papa to fetch the trunks," Mama said.

But Papa said, "Be glad Kirsten came with me. She's a brave girl, and a strong one. If she hadn't been along to help me, I'd never have found the cave or my way home."

Mama put her arm around Papa's waist. "I can believe that Kirsten is as brave as her papa. Come sit down here and rest your leg. I'll bring you some soup." She smiled at Kirsten. "Don't let yours get cold."

Anna and Lisbeth came to sit by Kirsten as she ate. "We were so frightened for you," Anna said. "Our papa wanted to go out in the storm to search for you, but Mama said he'd never find you on foot. We didn't know what to do! Were you scared?"

Kirsten sipped the thick soup. "I was scared. Then I was too busy to be scared anymore. Anyway, we're here now and we've got the trunk!" Under the table she gave Anna's hand a squeeze.

Anna put her head close to Kirsten's. "You don't want to have our surprise *now*, do you?"

Kirsten grinned. "This is Saint Lucia's Day and it's the perfect time," she whispered. "Saint Lucia is supposed to wake everyone at four in the morning. It must be about four now."

Lisbeth pulled her chair closer. "But how will we surprise everyone when they're all awake anyway?" she asked.

Kirsten lowered her voice even more. "When Lars and Uncle Olav bring the trunk in, Mama is sure to want to open it. I'll sneak the white dress out. In the meantime, you can get the crown and the tray of bread. When we're all ready, Miss Winston can tell everyone to shut their eyes. How will that be?"

"It's a grand idea!" Anna said. "I'll whisper to Miss Winston what she's supposed to do."

Lars and Uncle Olav carried the painted trunk into the middle of the cabin. When Uncle Olav lifted

the lid, the sweet scent of dried lavender filled the
air. Kirsten hurried to Mama's side.

Mama reached into the trunk and out came
Sari. Mama gave the doll a little hug and handed
her to Kirsten. "I know how much you missed
your doll, Kirsten. Last night I missed you and
Papa even more. Now we're all together again,
even Sari."

Kirsten took Sari in both hands and looked
at her closely in the flickering light. Sari was just a
rag doll with a faded face and a sun-bleached dress,
but she was Kirsten's very, very own. Kirsten

171

pressed Sari to her cheek.

"And here's Peter's clay whistle," Mama said.

Papa smiled and held his finger to his lips. Peter had fallen asleep beside him.

"This has been such a long night," Mama said gently to Papa. "You must be exhausted. Let's all get some sleep and finish unpacking the trunk later."

Anna leaned around the end of the trunk and tugged Kirsten's skirt. "*Do* something!" she whispered.

"At least find the sweaters from Mormor," Kirsten said to Mama. "And the pillow covers you wove for Aunt Inger. Unpack at least that much."

Mama didn't need to be urged. Piece by piece, she began to lift their precious things from the trunk. She handed them to Aunt Inger, who laid them on the table.

Kirsten watched for her chance. While Aunt Inger was exclaiming over the pillow covers, Kirsten slipped the white nightdress from the trunk and handed it to Anna. The red sash was right next to it, inside Peter's cap. Anna shoved them both under her sweater.

Out of the corner of her eye, Kirsten saw Lisbeth climbing down the ladder from the loft. She had their crown and the candles wrapped in a quilt.

The girls met at the far end of the kitchen by the door into the shed. "Here's the tray!" Lisbeth said. "And Miss Winston's ready. Quick, put on the dress, it's cold!"

Kirsten slipped off her dress and shawl and pulled the white nightdress over her head. Next came the red sash. Finally, Lisbeth fitted the crown on Kirsten's head and lit the candles.

"Oh, Kirsten!" Anna breathed. "You look like an angel!"

"We're almost ready now," Lisbeth said as she lit the candle on the tray.

Miss Winston came hurrying into the kitchen. "I told everyone to shut their eyes, then I turned down the lamps. Come now, they're waiting!"

Anna and Lisbeth scampered across the kitchen ahead of Kirsten. Kirsten lifted her head high, took a deep breath, and walked slowly, holding the tray of coffee and bread. The big room was dim except for the light of her crown. Kirsten paused in the doorway. She saw everyone waiting with their eyes

*"Saint Lucia invites you to breakfast!"*
*Kirsten said.*

174

closed, as Miss Winston had asked them to do.

"Saint Lucia invites you to breakfast!" Kirsten said.

For just a moment the room was still. The only sound was the crackle of the fire in the stove. Then the commotion began.

Peter rubbed his eyes. "Oh, it's Christmas time!" he cried. Everyone called out "Merry Christmas!" and "What a wonderful surprise!"

Kirsten looked around the room as she passed the Saint Lucia tray to her family. Mama's blue eyes were shining. Aunt Inger and Uncle Olav were smiling with pleasure. Peter and Lars grinned and munched their bread. Miss Winston squeezed Anna's hand.

"Is this what it was like last Christmas in Sweden?" Lisbeth asked Kirsten as she handed Papa a mug of coffee.

Kirsten thought a moment about how much she'd loved the home she'd left behind in Sweden. Then she smiled at the cousins she liked so well. How happy she'd been tonight when she and Papa had finally found their way back to this new home, which was brightly lit for them in the dark.

"It's almost the same, but this year I think it's even better," she told Lisbeth. "Yes, it *is* a better Christmas. I think it's the best one of all."

FOR MY MOTHER,
NADINA FOWLER

# 1854
# HAPPY BIRTHDAY, KIRSTEN!

*A Springtime Story*

# CHAPTER
## ONE
—
# TORNADO!

"Hit your rug harder!" Anna called to Kirsten. "Look, I can make more dust fly than you can!"

"It makes me sneeze," Kirsten said. But she liked smacking the rag carpets that Mama and Aunt Inger had draped over the line. She grinned as she slapped the dirt out with a small branch from the maple tree.

Anna held her branch with both hands. Because she was only eight, the youngest of the girls, she'd been given the smallest rug. The tip of her nose was as pink as a cherry blossom from the sun and the work.

After the long winter the clothes, bedding, and

rugs were full of dirt and soot, but Kirsten and Anna laughed and chattered as they beat the rugs. Lisbeth called "Hello!" as she brought bed linens from the big house to where Mama and Aunt Inger were doing the laundry. They were all so glad it was warm enough to be outside.

The Larsons' first winter in America had been bitterly cold, but at last the deep snows of Minnesota melted. Now May greened the farm Kirsten's family shared with Uncle Olav and Aunt Inger. Papa, Lars, and Uncle Olav were working the fields so they could plant wheat and corn. As soon as the seed was in the ground, the men would raise a new barn. That would be wonderful, Kirsten thought—a big new barn and a barn-raising party. But first there was so much work to be done.

Kirsten sneezed again and stopped to wipe her nose on the corner of her apron. The strong wind off the prairie whipped her skirt around her legs and pulled Anna's braids straight back from her head. It fanned the flames under the steaming laundry kettle where Mama and Aunt Inger stirred the sheets.

As Peter brought the cows in to be milked, his

cap blew off his head and tumbled across the barn lot. Mama scooped up the cap as it rolled to her feet, then looked at the sky in alarm.

Kirsten looked, too. All day the sun had shone, but now the sky was getting dark as though night were coming early. Mama waved Kirsten to her side. She put her wet, warm hand on Kirsten's shoulder. "Those black clouds worry me," Mama said.

Aunt Inger shaded her eyes to study the horizon. "Another tornado might be coming," she said. "Last spring a tornado ripped up the woodlot and almost took that old barn. We should go into the root cellar to be safe."

Even as Aunt Inger spoke, the wind blew several shingles off the roof of the little barn. "Get your brother and your cousins, Kirsten," Mama said. "Hurry!"

The wind shoved Kirsten as she ran to the barn lot. "Come quickly!" she called to Lisbeth and Anna. "That might be a tornado!" The pine trees thrashed, the tall grass flattened, and the wind howled as black clouds sped toward the farm. If a tornado touched down here, it could destroy the house and the cabin

*"Get your brother and your cousins, Kirsten," Mama said.*
*"Another tornado might be coming."*

and the barn and everything in them. It could carry away the pieces of the new barn that hadn't even been put up yet. Kirsten grabbed Peter's hand. "A tornado! We have to get underground to be safe! Come to the root cellar!"

No one had to be told twice to hide from a tornado. Peter picked up the gray cat, Missy, and ran after Kirsten. Mama was already at the back of the big house, opening the door to the root cellar. Anna and Lisbeth scrambled in like prairie dogs into a burrow. Aunt Inger came with a lantern and the family Bible in her arms. Right behind her ran Miss Winston, the schoolteacher who was staying with the Larsons. She held a quilt over her head and shoulders like a cloak.

Peter skidded into the root cellar with Kirsten right behind him. Then Mama and Miss Winston crowded in, and Aunt Inger dragged the door shut behind her and bolted it tightly.

"Where are Lars and Papa and Uncle Olav?" Kirsten asked.

"They're helping at the Peterson farm today, but don't worry. The men will lie down in a ditch if they see a funnel cloud coming," Aunt Inger said.

"Here, turn over a bucket and sit down." She lit the lantern and set it by her feet.

Everyone huddled together shoulder to shoulder in the little room dug out of the earth under the house. Last fall the root cellar had been packed full of potatoes, turnips, carrots, beets, and apples. During the winter the families had eaten almost all the vegetables. Now there were only a few wrinkled apples left. Aunt Inger picked them up and handed them around. "These will have to be our lunch," she said. "We can't go out until the danger is past."

Aunt Inger held the family Bible in her lap—it was the most important thing the Larsons owned. Every night Uncle Olav or Papa read from it. In the front of the Bible the names and important dates for everyone in the whole family were written. Kirsten liked to read her own birthday there:

*Kirsten Larson, born June 8, 1845, Ryd, Sweden*

In a month she would be ten years old.

Kirsten was too nervous to eat the apple Aunt Inger had given her. Outside, the wind roared and howled like the train that had brought her family across the country to their new home. What would they do if the tornado blew their cabin away? And Mama was going to have a baby soon—where would the baby be born if they didn't have a home? Kirsten pressed against Mama's side.

Miss Winston pulled her quilt from her head and smoothed her hair. "In Maine we never ever had a tornado. No one will believe me when I write home about these dangers!" But she smiled to show them that a ship captain's daughter knew how to be brave.

Anna touched the corner of Miss Winston's quilt. "Couldn't you find your cloak?" she asked. Anna was never too scared to be curious.

"I never thought about my cloak! I just knew I had to save my quilt, so I took it and ran." Miss Winston sat up straight like a lady and smoothed the quilt in her lap. "Every time I look at my quilt, it's like getting a letter from home."

"You were right to save it," Aunt Inger said. "It's beautiful!"

Kirsten had often seen the brightly colored quilt on Miss Winston's bed, but she'd never looked at it closely. Now she leaned forward to study it. It was

white, and covered with designs that looked like
wreaths of flowers. Each design was made from
small pieces of fabric. The whole quilt was sewn with
tiny, perfect stitches, the kind of stitches Mama was
teaching Kirsten to make.

"It must have taken a long time to sew," Lisbeth
said. She was twelve, and her sewing was already
like a grown woman's.

Anna shuddered when the wind huffed at the
door. "Did you make your quilt, Miss Winston?" she
asked in a small voice.

"Oh, no! Shall I tell you how this quilt was
made?" Miss Winston said.

Anna nudged Kirsten's foot with hers, because
Miss Winston never missed a chance to teach a
lesson. "Yes, please," Anna said.

"It did take a long time to sew," Miss Winston
said proudly. "My mother and my aunts and cousins
and my sister made this quilt for me. They gave it
to me to remember them by when I left home." She
pointed to the flower designs in the quilt.
"The pink cloth in the center of this flower
is from my sister's old apron. The cloth
in this green leaf is from a dress of my

mother's. The yellow cloth for the flower petals came from a dress I wore as a baby."

It was hard for Kirsten to imagine Miss Winston as a baby, but she liked the quilt's lively colors. They made her think of the wildflowers in the meadow.

"Everyone who helped make this quilt signed her name to it," Miss Winston said. "It's a friendship quilt." Her eyes had a faraway look, as though she were gazing at her friends and family back in Maine instead of the dirt walls of the damp root cellar.

"Do you think you could teach us to sew a quilt?" Kirsten asked. Whenever she admired something, she wanted to do it herself.

"Yes, could you?" Lisbeth echoed.

Miss Winston raised her eyebrows. "Haven't I taught you sums and reading and recitation and penmanship? Of course I can teach you to make a quilt! A big one like mine would be difficult, but you could each make a small square. I have some white muslin in my trunk. I'll cut three pieces for the background."

Anna nudged Kirsten's foot again as the girls

looked at each other excitedly. "But what can we use for making the designs?" Kirsten asked.

"You'll need only small bits of cloth for that," Miss Winston said. "Just scraps will do."

"We can use my worn-out kerchief," Anna said.

"And scraps from the ragbag," Lisbeth added.

"My apron can't be patched any more. We could cut it up for scraps," Kirsten said.

Mama put her hand on Kirsten's knee. "You don't have time for fancy sewing," she said. "Remember, I need all your help to make clothes for the baby." She patted her big belly to remind Kirsten that it wouldn't be long now until they'd need the baby things.

Kirsten sighed. It was tiresome to hem shirts and diapers for the baby Mama was expecting. Why did a baby need so many diapers? Surely three or four would be enough.

"But quilting trains the hand and eye," Miss Winston said sternly, as though Mama were one of her pupils, too. "And a quilt is so practical. Mine is wonderfully warm."

Mama looked doubtful. Quilting was something

new to her. The Swedish women wove their blankets and bedcoverings on looms.

"Maybe Lisbeth and I could learn and teach you when you have time, Kirsten," Anna said.

"I bet you'll still be able to sew just before bedtime," Lisbeth said. "And at school we can sew during recess. I know the other girls would like to do it, too."

"Sewing at recess, what a good idea!" Miss Winston said. "After you walk about and take deep breaths, I'm sure there will be a little time left for sewing. Where there's a will there's always a way."

She wrapped her quilt around her shoulders again.

The gray cat jumped from Peter's lap and curled around Kirsten's ankles. Missy was going to have kittens soon and didn't like to be fussed over now. But Kirsten felt comforted when she petted the cat, so she stroked Missy's soft head. "I'll sew the baby things so fast that I know I'll have some time," she told Lisbeth and Anna.

"It's decided, then!" Lisbeth said. "We'll learn to make a quilt."

"Who knows what these girls will learn next!" Aunt Inger said to Mama. Then she cocked her head. While they'd been talking, the wind had died down. "I think it might be safe to go out now," she said. "Let's look."

She lifted the heavy bolt. The small door swung open onto a patch of sky as blue as one of the pieces in Miss Winston's quilt. All the rugs and covers had blown off the lines, and a few shingles had blown off the rooftops. Broken branches littered the barn lot. But both houses and the old barn stood safe in the clearing among the pines.

Mama let out a long sigh, as though she'd been holding her breath. "Thank God that this danger has passed us by," she said. They crept out of the root cellar like bears out of a cave, into the fresh air.

## CHAPTER
## TWO
---
# NEW BABIES

School started again for the summer, and all the girls gathered at recess every day to sew. Kirsten liked to lean against the sun-warmed logs of the schoolhouse and chatter with her friends. They had traded scraps of cloth so that everyone could make a colorful design on a square of white muslin. The designs they made from the bits of cloth slowly grew in their hands the way wild violets bloomed on the prairie.

Mary Stewart, whose family had come to Minnesota from Boston, was making the fanciest design. Mary had worked on a quilt before, so when Miss Winston wasn't there to give directions, she

194

helped the others sew difficult corners and curves. She had beautiful curly brown hair and a squinched-up face like a sleepy puppy's.

Today Mary was showing Kirsten how to make a sharp corner. Her curls brushed Kirsten's braids as they bent over a small piece of blue cloth. "This is a piece of linen my mother wove," Kirsten said. "There was just a tiny bit left after she made a shirt for Papa. Now all she makes are baby clothes. She's making little caps from an old pillowcase."

Mary wet her finger and knotted a piece of thread. "Last year my Aunt Sadie had twins. Only one of the babies lived, and Aunt Sadie died after they were born."

Kirsten made herself concentrate on Mary's quick fingers and the flashing needle. She didn't want to think that Mama was in danger.

"My mother took Aunt Sadie's baby to raise. We call her my little sister, but she's really my cousin. She never knew her real mother, of course," Mary went on, her lips pursed over her sewing.

Kirsten pricked her finger on her needle and sucked hard at the hurt place. Everyone seemed to know stories of mothers or babies who had died

*"Last year my Aunt Sadie had twins," said Mary.*
*"Only one of the babies lived."*

196

here on the frontier. To think of something happening to Mama made Kirsten want to cry. It was better not to think of that. It was much better to think about the pretty designs they were making.

Anna had left the sewing circle to ask Miss Winston to untangle her thread. Now she came running back. Gladly, Kirsten made a place for Anna to sit between her and Mary. Anna pulled her quilt square from her apron pocket. "Honestly, isn't Miss Winston the nicest teacher ever? I'll be sorry when she has to leave Powderkeg School."

Kirsten was startled. She thought Miss Winston would be with them always, like family. "Why would she want to leave?" Kirsten asked.

"Teachers always move on," Mary said. "I've been at this school for four years and we've had four different teachers. Miss Winston is the only nice one."

Anna picked a little white flower that bloomed in the shelter of the log school and held it to her nose. "Miss Winston likes it here. She often says so."

"I hope she stays!" Kirsten said. She wished that everything would stay just as it was now.

The morning light was sweet and clear, the woods were green again, and they were all happy to have Miss Winston with them. If only Mama felt better— that was the one thing Kirsten would change. These days Mama was as nervous and irritable as Missy, the gray cat.

"If Miss Winston does leave, maybe we could add our squares to her quilt. Then she'd remember us, too," Anna said. "I can imagine her saying, 'This piece of brown calico is Anna's. This blue linen is Kirsten's.'"

"And, 'This red cotton is Mary's,'" Mary added quickly. "But Miss Winston's quilt is finished. When she showed it to us, I saw the fancy border."

Kirsten had an idea. "We could make another quilt for Miss Winston. And we could all sign our names to it, just the way her family did. Then when she looks at it, she'll think of all of us."

Anna smiled right away. She jumped to her feet and pranced around the circle, lifting her knees like a little pony. "That's a grand idea!" she said.

But Mary frowned. "It takes a long time to make a quilt. We can't make one in a rush."

Kirsten pressed her lips together tightly. Oh, she knew Mary was right. It had taken several days just to cut out a design. Sewing it to the background was taking even longer. And making all the tiny quilting stitches would surely take weeks. Now that there was so much work to do at home, Kirsten had no time to work on her design before bed. Some days Mama's back ached so badly that Kirsten had to stay home from school to help her bake and cook. On those days, Kirsten didn't even get to sew at recess.

Still, Kirsten wouldn't give up her plan to make a quilt. "We could sew all of our squares together and make a small one," she said. "If we worked fast, we could finish it before the summer term is over."

"I think we should try," Lisbeth agreed in her slow voice that meant she was serious. She liked to think things through, so when she said they'd try, Kirsten thought the quilt was as good as finished.

But Mary sat back on her heels. She shook her brown curls like a wet dog shaking off water. "No, no, no!"

Kirsten was surprised. "Why not at least try?" she asked.

Mary folded her arms and shook her head again. "You don't understand. Being finished with the quilt isn't the best part," she said firmly. "*Making* the quilt is the best part. Anyway, that's what I like best— sewing it, all of us together."

Kirsten looked at Mary with new respect. Of course Mary was right. When the quilt was finished, the fun of working together would be over. And to be working and talking with her friends made Kirsten happy. "Yes," she said. "You're right, Mary."

Anna stood behind Kirsten. "I love your design!" she said. "It looks just like a heart."

"It's really a flower," Kirsten said. "I want it to look like the flowers Mama gave me to wear in my hair when I turned eight. We didn't celebrate my birthday when I turned nine. We were on our way from Sweden then."

"Then I'm sure you'll have a big celebration this year," Mary said. "Ten is a much more important birthday than nine, anyway."

Kirsten licked her thread and threaded her needle. Maybe she wouldn't celebrate her birthday this year, either. Maybe Mama had forgotten about

her birthday. Mama had so much work to do for
the new baby, and so much on her mind these days.
Kirsten wanted to remind Mama, but she thought
it was better not to bother her until after the baby
was born. It was better just to help out all she could
and pray that Mama would be well.

*Helping out* meant more and more work for
Kirsten. The cows gave more milk in the spring, so
there was cheese to make and butter to churn. The
chickens were laying again, and Kirsten had to feed
them and gather eggs. She picked berries and greens
to eat, too, and cooked breakfast and dinner when
Mama wasn't able to be on her feet. Every night
when her chores were done, Kirsten went straight to
bed and fell asleep. And as soon as she woke in the
morning, she started on that day's tasks. There was
no time for sewing now.

One morning, as Kirsten was milking the cows
with Aunt Inger, Lisbeth burst into the barn. "Come
see Missy's new kittens!" she cried.

"What are you doing here, Lisbeth? You're
supposed to be cooking breakfast," Aunt Inger said

sternly. "The men will be in from the fields soon. They'll be hungry."

"I *was* cooking. Then Anna brought the eggs in, and she said that Missy was having her kittens. So I came out to see them. They're so small they look like mice." Lisbeth wiped her hand on her apron and made herself talk more slowly. "Kirsten, maybe you could come take a quick peek. The kittens have made a home in a pile of straw."

Kirsten looked at Aunt Inger, who nodded but didn't smile. Milk hissed into her bucket in two white streams. "Go on then, but be fast about it," Aunt Inger said. "We've still got two cows waiting."

Kirsten jumped up and followed Lisbeth. The sun was just rising, as pink as a primrose. The scent of lilacs and freshly turned earth was in the air. In the barn lot, Anna and Peter crouched beside a pile of straw near a huge wooden beam for the new barn. There was Missy, curled around her five baby kittens.

Missy licked and licked the kittens, which crawled blindly against her belly to look for milk.

Two of the kittens were black and white, two were gray and white, and the smallest one was gray, just like Missy. The gray kitten was so small it couldn't squeeze in to find a place to nurse. Instead, it bumped up against the beam, then against Missy's hind leg.

"That one's so little it will never live," Peter said. He'd heard Uncle Olav say that about one of the piglets.

"Be quiet, Peter," Kirsten said. "You don't know everything." She tried to guide the tiny gray kitten to its mother. But the kitten couldn't find its way.

"I think it has a chance," Lisbeth said. "Though sometimes those very little ones aren't strong enough to make it."

Kirsten touched the gray kitten's stomach with the tip of her finger. The kitten's heart beat like the flutter of a butterfly wing. Its tiny mouth closed around her fingertip. Kirsten moved the kitten closer to Missy. "Oh, yes, that kitten will make it," Kirsten whispered. "You'll see."

"You like that one best, don't you?" Peter said.

Kirsten nodded.

"Well, I like that black and white one," Peter said. He liked the puppies that were the toughest and the calves that were the biggest, too.

"I've got to finish milking with Aunt Inger," Kirsten said. "Peter, you make sure the gray kitten doesn't get lost in the grass, will you?"

Peter stood up and shoved his hands into his pockets the way their big brother Lars did. "Missy will take care of her kittens. She doesn't need help."

But Kirsten wasn't sure. That gray kitten was so very, very small. She leaned down to pet it one more time and whispered, "Be careful. Don't wander away or a hawk might get you. Drink lots of milk. I'll come back to see you later." She wanted to stay to guard it, but instead she ran back to the barn to help Aunt Inger.

# BIG ENOUGH

"Kirsten! Kirsten!" Mama was calling from their cabin. It was late morning, and Kirsten and Lisbeth were straining cheese curds in the shed next to the big house. Kirsten put down the strainer and went to see what Mama wanted.

In the dim cabin, Mama sat on the edge of the bed. Her hands were pressed against her big belly. There was sweat on her forehead, and she looked worried. "Where's your Aunt Inger?" she asked.

"She took a pot of soup to the Petersons because they've been so sick. She'll be back by noontime," Kirsten said.

"And where's Papa?"

206

"He and Uncle Olav are helping Mr. Peterson finish his planting." Kirsten looked at her mother curiously. Why was Mama asking all these questions? She knew as well as Kirsten what work had to be done today. She was the one who had told Kirsten and Lisbeth to strain cheese curds.

"They'll be back soon, won't they?" Mama asked.

"Yes, Mama. They'll be back in time for lunch. Is something wrong?"

Mama patted the bed beside her. "Sit with me for a little while and keep me company. I think the baby is going to be born sooner than I expected. Maybe even today."

Kirsten's heart sped up and her mouth went dry. "Shouldn't I go fetch Aunt Inger to help you?"

"She'll be back soon. Just let me lie down and rest," Mama said.

Kirsten got the extra blanket and put it over Mama. Then she sat down beside her on the bed. Mama laced her fingers through Kirsten's. "Do you know what I thought about when I woke this morning?" Mama asked. Her eyes were a soft blue like the morning sky.

"What did you think about, Mama?"

Mama squeezed Kirsten's hand. "I remembered the day you were born, Kirsten. I remembered how my mother came to help me. Mrs. Hanson came, too. She helped all of us when we had babies. It was this time of year, late spring. New leaves were on the big maple tree outside the door. Then you were born, and Mrs. Hanson cleaned you and wrapped you in a blanket and put you in my arms. You were a red-faced little thing with white fuzz for hair. But I thought you were beautiful. I was so very, very happy because I wanted a daughter so much."

Kirsten put her head on her mother's shoulder. "Well, here I am," she said.

"Yes, here you are!" Mama smoothed the hair back from Kirsten's forehead. "And I was also thinking," Mama went on, stroking Kirsten's head, "that your birthday will be two weeks from this very day. June eighth. I'll never forget the day you were born."

So Mama did remember her birthday. How foolish Kirsten had been to think she would forget.

Suddenly, Mama squeezed Kirsten's hand extra

hard. Kirsten sat up straight. "Are you all right, Mama?"

"This baby wants to be born whether we're ready or not. We'd better not wait for Inger to come home. You'd better go fetch her, and Papa, too."

"Can't I help you here?" Kirsten asked. Her heart was racing.

"Get Lisbeth to stay with me," Mama said. "You go for Aunt Inger and Papa. Will you do that for me?" Mama wiped the sweat from her face with a corner of the blanket.

"I'll take Blackie. I'll ride as fast as an Indian, Mama! I'll be right back with Aunt Inger and Papa! I promise!"

As Kirsten ran across the yard, she called, "Lisbeth, Mama's baby is coming and she needs you! Go quickly!" Then Kirsten dashed to the barn, grabbed Blackie's bridle, and chased him in from the pasture. "We have to hurry, Blackie!" she said as she pressed the bit between the horse's teeth. She climbed up the fence and onto his back.

Blackie liked to run. When Kirsten turned him into the lane and kicked him, he took off like a prairie fire. Kirsten leaned forward, and Blackie's mane whipped her face. She held on to his mane and the reins, and guided him with her knees. It wasn't far to the Petersons' cabin, maybe only two or three miles.

"Come on!" Kirsten urged the horse. Blackbirds swooped up from the fields as they passed. Blackie's hooves on the dirt lane pounded like a second heartbeat. "Let Mama be all right!" Kirsten prayed. "Please, let her be all right!"

Kirsten began calling, "Aunt Inger! Aunt Inger!" as she rode up to the Petersons' cabin. Aunt Inger was at the doorway in a moment.

"Is it your mama's time?" she asked.

"She says to come quickly. Oh, Aunt Inger, please go as fast as you can!"

But Aunt Inger was already on her way, running more than walking, taking the shortcut across the fields. "Your father and the others are near the creek," she called over her shoulder. "And don't worry. Your mama is strong and healthy."

Kirsten couldn't help but worry. She turned Blackie to guide him down to the creek. Blackie couldn't gallop on this rocky path, but he trotted as if he knew they were on an important errand. Pine

*"Oh, Aunt Inger," Kirsten said,*
*"please go as fast as you can!"*

branches switched Kirsten's arms and shoulders. She ducked low along Blackie's warm back, riding the way the Indians rode their ponies.

Then they were in the plowed field and Kirsten saw Papa. "Papa! Mama wants you!" she yelled as she galloped across the field. "The baby's coming!"

"Is it that much of a hurry?" he said.

"Yes! You take the horse, Papa."

Papa gave Kirsten's shoulder a squeeze. He said, "You're a good helper, Kirsten," as he hoisted himself up on the horse's back.

Uncle Olav called, "Good luck!" as Papa took off for the cabin. Kirsten and Uncle Olav followed on foot.

"Let's run!" Kirsten said. "I want to help Mama, too!"

"Walking will get us there fast enough, Kirsten," Uncle Olav said kindly. "You're too young to be in the cabin anyway. Inger and your father will do what's needed for your mama. You wait with Lisbeth and Anna at our house. There's plenty for you to do there."

So Kirsten went back to the big house, where Lisbeth heated soup and sliced bread and cheese for the noon meal. But how could Kirsten eat when Mama was having the baby? She picked at her food. Waiting was so hard.

"We'd all better get on with what we have to do," Uncle Olav said after he finished his soup. "Babies come when they're ready. We can't hurry this one by worrying."

The afternoon crept along. Kirsten washed up the bowls and then fed the pigs and chickens. She was picking feathers from a wild turkey Lars had shot when she saw Aunt Inger in the doorway of the cabin. Aunt Inger waved her apron like a flag. And she was smiling!

Kirsten and Peter leaped like jackrabbits across the pasture. As they came to the door of the cabin, Kirsten took Peter's hand. He was trembling like a newborn calf. "Is Mama all right?" he blurted before Aunt Inger had a chance to say a word.

But Kirsten knew from Aunt Inger's smile that the news was good. "Come see for yourselves," Aunt Inger said and stood aside.

Kirsten and Peter tiptoed into the cabin. The sunlight made a path across the floor to the big bed where Mama lay.

213

She held out her hand to them. "Come see your little sister," she said.

There in the wooden cradle lay a little bundle in a blanket. Kirsten bent down. She saw a tiny pink face under a wisp of hair like yellow duck down.

"I thought a baby would be bigger," Peter said softly.

"Babies start out very small," Mama said. "But she's big enough." She reached up and ruffled his fair hair.

Peter grinned. "She's big enough," he repeated.

"Oh, Mama!" Kirsten breathed. Suddenly all of the extra energy went out of her. She wished she could just curl up on the bed beside Mama and rest, too.

"Now there are six of us," Mama said.

"More mouths to feed," Papa said. He was smiling his biggest smile. "But all six of us are safe and well, thank the Lord."

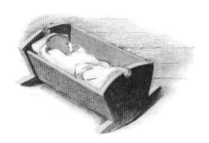

# PARTY PLANS

"How soon are we going to raise the barn?" Peter asked. These days he always said "we" when he talked about the men's work. Papa was even teaching him to split wood with the small axe.

Papa, Peter, and Lars sat at the table eating the rabbit stew Kirsten had made for their supper. "We plan to raise it a week from next Thursday, if the weather is good," Papa said. "The other farmers will come as soon as they've done their morning chores. They'll bring their families with them, of course. There will be nine men, plus Olav and Lars. That should be enough." Papa had explained several times how the men would pull up the big beams

215

and posts to make the barn. The beams were so long
and heavy that Kirsten couldn't imagine how they
would be raised. But it seemed that Papa and Uncle
Olav could do anything.

Kirsten dished up a serving of stew for Mama,
who rested in the bed with the baby. Mama wasn't
strong enough to work for very long yet, so Kirsten
did most of Mama's kitchen and farm chores. And
there were new chores, too. Several times each day,
Kirsten washed out the baby's diapers and hung
them to dry on the line outside.
With all her work, Kirsten had no
time to go to school. How lonely
it was on the farm when Anna and
Lisbeth were away all day. It seemed like years
since Kirsten had sat in that sunny spot behind the
schoolhouse, sewing with her friends. Every day
she was home, she imagined them working on their
squares without her. How she missed them and the
fun of making the quilt.

"Your friends from school will be here for the
barn raising," Mama said when she took her bowl
of stew from Kirsten. "They'll be coming with their
parents. Each family will bring food, and Inger is

216

going to make a huge kettle of venison stew for everyone."

That pleased Kirsten, though she didn't see how she'd have time to play with the other girls. She'd probably have to help Mama with the extra work.

"The families will be here all day, and after supper we'll have music and dancing," Mama went on. "I can't dance yet, but you and the others can." Mama didn't seem to mind about the dancing. She was smiling down at the baby who slept beside her.

Mama tugged Kirsten's braid. "I have something to ask you, dear."

Kirsten sighed. More work to do, she was sure. "Yes, Mama," she said obediently.

"Our barn raising will be on the day before your birthday. I thought you might like to do something special when your friends are here," Mama said. "You've done the work of two women lately, and you deserve a day to play."

Kirsten took Mama's hand. "A whole day with my friends?"

Mama smiled. "Your tenth birthday should be a day of your own. A day to celebrate and to have fun."

217

Kirsten thought about picking wildflowers and playing games. And maybe there would be a cake to share. A barn raising and a birthday celebration, too! "May I run tell Lisbeth and Anna about it?" she asked Mama.

Papa started to say something about washing up, but Mama said, "Dishes can wait."

"I'll be right back," Kirsten said and scooted out the door.

As Kirsten ran to the other house, a wood thrush called and another answered from the pines. A thrush's song had never seemed such a happy melody as it did this evening. Kirsten tapped on the door, and Anna and Lisbeth came outside with her.

"They're coming! And it will be my birthday and a party!" Kirsten cried.

Lisbeth wiped her hands on her apron and said, "Slow down. Start over. Who's coming?"

Kirsten caught her breath. "On the day the men raise the barn, all our friends from school will be here. Mama says I can celebrate my birthday that day!"

"That's grand!" Anna said. She jumped up and down, her braids bouncing.

Lisbeth grabbed Kirsten's hand and swung it. "A party! Oh, that's wonderful news!"

"Mama says we'll be together all day and evening," Kirsten said. "We could work on our quilt for Miss Winston, too!"

Anna said, "But it's not for Miss—"

"Hush, Anna!" Lisbeth said. "It would be a perfect chance to work on the quilt, and you know it."

Anna blushed. "That's what I meant," she said.

"I'm way behind the rest of you with my sewing," Kirsten said. "It doesn't seem like I'm doing my part. But maybe I can catch up by then."

Anna put her arm around Kirsten's waist and looked up with a smile. "Oh, everyone knows you can't work on the quilt because you have to help your mama. It doesn't matter, truly it doesn't."

"It matters to me!" Kirsten said. "I miss the fun of doing it. And I miss being with all of you, too!" she blurted.

"On the day of your party, we'll sew as much as you want to," Lisbeth said.

Anna let go of Kirsten and hugged herself instead. "Oh, I can't wait for the surprise!"

"She means she can't wait for your party," Lisbeth said.

"I just wish I were going to be ten like you are, Kirsten!" Anna added.

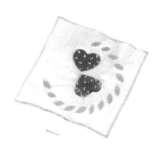

# FRIENDS COME
# AROUND

"Pick as many daisies as you can!"
Anna told everyone. "We're going
to make daisy chains." All eight girls
fanned out across the meadow. It was the day of the
barn raising and they were picking wildflowers.

The day was clear and sunny, and Kirsten's
spirits swooped and soared like the bluebirds. She
stopped to look across the meadow to where the
men were working on the barn. Just after sunrise
they'd begun to haul the big beams up with strong
ropes, and by late morning there was the outline
of a barn where there had been only open sky. The
prairie didn't seem so wide with the new barn
there. Kirsten hoped Missy had kept her kittens

out of the way of the workers. Later, she'd look for the kittens. Now she buried her nose in the sweet-smelling bouquet she held.

When the girls had picked all the flowers they could carry, they took them back to Aunt Inger's house and decorated the big room with daisy chains. Then they sat outside under the dappled shade of the maple tree to sew. Kirsten had not finished the design on her square, but the other girls had finished theirs. When they laid them together on the grass, the squares made a lively pattern of blues, reds, greens, browns, and white. Mary arranged them. "We'll use a running stitch to join the squares. This part will go quickly," she said.

Kirsten hoped it wouldn't go too quickly. She knelt with her friends in a circle, chattering away as they joined their squares to make the top of a small quilt.

After the noon meal, the girls took up their sewing again. By the middle of the afternoon, they finished stitching the top of their quilt to a plain backing.

"This quilt isn't as large or heavy as the one

*Kirsten knelt with her friends in a circle,
chattering away as they joined their squares.*

Miss Winston has," Kirsten said.

"It's a summer coverlet," Mary explained. "No one had an extra blanket to sew between the layers."

"I'm sure Miss Winston will like it though," Kirsten added.

Anna giggled and hid her smile behind her hand.

"Anyway, I think it's lovely!" Kirsten went on. Now that she was with her friends again, she felt more strongly how much she'd missed them.

Mary was folding up the quilt when Aunt Inger called from the doorway, "Aren't you girls ready for some sweets?"

Everyone shouted "Yes!" at the same time and ran into the house. "Let me get Mama," Kirsten said. But Mama was already coming from the kitchen, carrying a heart-shaped cake. Kirsten caught her breath with pleasure.

Miss Winston clapped her hands and pretended to be stern. "Everyone must sit in a circle," she said.

"Happy birthday, Kirsten!" Lisbeth said. She placed a wreath of flowers on Kirsten's head. The blossoms tickled Kirsten's ears through her long hair. "Thank you, Lisbeth," she said.

"You look beautiful," Anna said.

"Now the cake!" Mama called.

When everyone was munching, Aunt Inger said, "I have something for your birthday, Kirsten." She gave Kirsten a small package.

"New hair ribbons! Pink is my favorite color. Thank you, Aunt Inger!" Kirsten said.

Now Mama stepped forward. "And I made you something pretty, for dress up." She handed Kirsten a white apron with fancy trim around the edges.

"Oh, Mama, it's lovely!" Kirsten said. "But when did you have time to make this?"

Miss Winston leaned close and whispered, "Where there's a will, there's always a way."

"I could wear this tonight at the barn-raising dance, couldn't I?"

"You may wear it and the hair ribbons," Mama smiled.

As Aunt Inger spooned strawberries into bowls and covered them with fresh cream, Mary stood up, brushed crumbs off her skirt, and straightened her shoulders importantly. "Now *we* have something to give to Kirsten." She crossed the room, picked up the little quilt they had just finished sewing, and proudly handed it to Kirsten. "Happy birthday, Kirsten. From all of us," she said.

Kirsten blinked. "Oh, thank you! But why are you giving this to me? It was for Miss Winston," she added in a whisper.

"I told the girls that one quilt is enough for anyone," Miss Winston said with a smile.

"And we're giving this one to you because you missed out on the fun of making it," Lisbeth explained. "We want you to know we didn't forget you, even when you weren't with us."

Anna took a corner of the quilt and spread it on the table. "See these plain squares? We put the plain ones in so we could write our names on them. Then it will be a friendship quilt, just like Miss Winston's."

Miss Winston took a quill pen and an inkpot from her school bag. "You must use your best handwriting," she directed the girls. "I don't want to see a single ink spot or smudge on this quilt."

Kirsten stroked the edge of her quilt as each girl

226

took a turn signing her name on one of the plain squares. When all of the squares had been signed, Miss Winston wrote on the border of the quilt with her most beautiful writing:

*For Kirsten Larson on her tenth birthday*

♥

It was late afternoon when the women began preparing supper. The men had finished raising the roof beams for the new barn, and now they used the extra boards to make wide tables. The girls set out pitchers of water and beer, and the women opened their baskets and laid out cheeses, breads, jam, butter, hams, roasted chickens, and cakes. The big pot of venison stew gave off a spicy scent. Everyone sat down to enjoy the feast, chatting and calling to one another as the sun began to set. Kirsten was almost too happy to be hungry. There would never be another day like this one, she was sure.

As the sky darkened, lanterns were hung on the crossbeams of the barn. Some of the men took out fiddles, and the barn-raising dance began. Under the lanterns, the grownups danced to the tunes. Yankee tunes, German tunes, and Swedish tunes followed each other like the swirling dancers. The children made circle dances of their own around the edges. The full moon shone down through the open rafters like the biggest lantern of all.

Kirsten was skipping with Anna when she felt Papa's hand on her shoulder. "Come on, ten-year-old," Papa said in his deep voice. "This is your birthday dance with me."

The fiddlers were playing a spinning waltz. Papa clasped Kirsten firmly around her waist, she hung on to his shoulders, and they joined the grownups in the center of the new barn. Kirsten smelled Papa's good, clean sweat and the smell of new wood. Sometimes her feet left the floor when Papa swung her around, and the faces of the other dancers spun by like a moving daisy chain, but Papa guided her and kept her steady.

When the waltz was over, Kirsten was so excited she felt dizzy. Or maybe she'd just whirled around too many times. She left Papa and the crowd and went to rest on the back of one of the wagons. As she sat quietly in the moonlight, she

*"Come on, ten-year-old," Papa said.*
*"This is your birthday dance with me."*

saw Missy moving her kittens into the new barn.
One by one, Missy lifted the kittens between the
posts and into a dark corner. Kirsten counted four
kittens. Where was the fifth one? Where was the
little gray kitten?

Kirsten jumped up and went to look for it in
the pile of straw where she'd seen them all before.

She got down on her hands and knees and
searched. Then she heard a tiny mew. There
was the gray kitten! But Missy didn't
seem to be coming back. Maybe she had
given up on this kitten.

Kirsten took the kitten into her hand. She cupped
it against her cheek and then snuggled it into the
deep pocket of her new apron. She could feed it
cow's milk, and it would grow strong. She would
care for it, and it would live.

As Kirsten walked back to the new barn, the
crowd began coming out. The men hitched their
horses to the wagons. The women gathered up their
baskets and sleepy children. Again and again, Papa
and Uncle Olav thanked their neighbors. The women
and girls hugged, then waved. "Good-bye! Good-
bye! Good night!" echoed across the dark fields as

the wagons pulled away.

Kirsten headed up to their cabin. When she opened the door, there was Mama, rocking the new baby in her cradle.

"Aren't you weary, Kirsten?" Mama asked. "Peter tried to stay awake, but you can see he fell asleep in his clothes."

Kirsten pulled her little stool next to Mama's chair. She liked the steady creak, creak the rocking cradle made. She took the kitten out of her pocket and showed it to Mama. "Missy left this one behind. I'm going to feed it."

"When it wakes up, dip the corner of a hankie into milk and let it suck," Mama suggested. "Tomorrow we'll see if Missy wants her little one back."

It was good to be in the quiet cabin with Mama. But Kirsten was much too excited to be able to sleep yet. She put the kitten in her lap, then laid her friendship quilt over her knees and tucked it close. After a moment the kitten began to purr. Kirsten picked up the quilt square she hadn't been able to finish and started to sew her design again.

"What will you do with that square?" Mama

asked in a sleepy voice.

Kirsten thought a moment. "I think I'll begin a quilt for our baby. It will take a long time to make, but that doesn't matter. I should have it finished before the weather gets cold again."

"What a special gift *that* will be," Mama said.

Kirsten smiled at Mama. "Remember you told me how glad you were to have a daughter? Is it better to have two daughters?"

Mama leaned to kiss Kirsten's cheek. "It's very good to have two daughters. But you are my only, only Kirsten. Happy birthday, dear."

FOR MY MOTHER,
NADINA FOWLER

*1854*

# KIRSTEN
# SAVES
# THE DAY

*A Summer Story*

# THE BEE TREE

"We need enough fish for our supper, and for Uncle Olav's family, too," Mama told Kirsten and her little brother Peter. "That's fish for nine hungry people. Can you catch that many?" She handed them fishing poles and a willow basket to put the fish in when they caught them.

"Yes, Mama! We can catch all the fish you need," Kirsten said. "The stream is full of trout." The June day was warm and sunny, and she was eager to be on her way.

"Good! And take care of Peter," Mama added, looking straight at Kirsten. "The last time he went fishing with you, he chased a skunk."

Peter made a face. "I only did that once!" he said and picked up a small basket filled with the crickets they would use for bait.

With the baby on her shoulder, Mama walked with Kirsten and Peter to the path that crossed the meadow. "Remember, you've got bare feet, so watch for snakes," Mama said as they hurried ahead of her. "And keep a lookout for bears. Don't take any foolish chances."

"We'll be careful!" Kirsten called.

"Do you have your whistle?" Mama called back.

"Yes, Mama, I'll blow it if anything happens." Kirsten waved the wooden whistle her brother Lars had carved for her, then grinned at Peter. "Mama worries too much," she whispered.

Peter swung the bait basket. "Papa says that mothers are *supposed* to worry. Let's run, Kirsten!"

As they ran toward the stream the black-and-white puppy, Caro, dashed down the path after them. The pup leaped against Peter's legs and then Kirsten's skirt. "We should chase Caro back home," Kirsten said. "He might steal our fish, and Mama is counting on us to get enough for supper."

Peter knelt and scratched Caro's head. The pup swiped Peter's ear with his pink tongue. "Please let Caro come with us!" he said. "He likes the stream, just like we do."

Caro cocked his head and gazed up at Kirsten. He was white with one black ear and black spots. "You're such a cute pup," Kirsten said. She turned to her brother. "But Peter, you know Caro will chase anything, even a snake. If he comes with us, you'll have to look after him. Can you take care of him and catch fish, too?"

"I'll take care of him!" Peter said. "I promise!"

So Caro tagged along. His white tail waved like a goose feather as he bounded through the grass, chasing blackbirds.

At the stream, Peter rolled up his pants. Kirsten tucked her skirt into the waistband of her apron and turned up the bottoms of her pantalettes. Caro splashed into the water to lap up a drink.

"Peter, call Caro!" Kirsten said. "He'll scare away the fish."

Peter whistled, and the pup jumped onto the bank and shook off a shower of drops. "See? He's a good puppy," Peter said. "He minds me, and I won't let him cause trouble." He handed Kirsten a cricket to bait her hook.

Kirsten waded slowly into the stream until the cool water came to her knees. The pebbles under her feet were soft with moss, and tiny fish tickled her ankles. She shivered with pleasure as she dropped her line into the water. She was glad the heavy work of spring cleaning and planting was over. Now, after school and on free days, there was happier work to do. Like fishing! She thought there must be more trout here in Minnesota than anywhere in the world.

Peter baited his hook and followed Kirsten. Sweat ran from his yellow hair down his sunburned cheeks. "I wish we could swim instead of catch fish," he said. "Don't you wish we could go swimming, Kirsten?"

"I'd rather go fishing every single day!" Kirsten said. She squinted at Peter in the hot sun. Sweat ran down her forehead, too. "But I wish I had a straw hat like the ones Lisbeth and Anna wear. This sunbonnet is too warm." She loosened the sunbonnet ties under her chin, but still the damp cotton hat clung to her head.

Peter's willow pole dipped. "I've got a bite!" he cried. He pulled in a trout and held it for Kirsten to see.

The trout was dark green with orange and blue markings. Kirsten thought it was beautiful. "It's too small to keep, though," she said.

"But it's the only one we've caught, and we need lots and lots for dinner," Peter said.

"Papa says to throw the little ones back and let them grow," Kirsten reminded him. "We'll catch bigger fish in the deep pool upstream."

Peter tossed the fish back into the clear water, and they took their baskets and poles and waded upstream. Caro followed on the bank, sniffing at deer tracks.

Sure enough, the quiet pool was full of trout. It seemed that every time Kirsten or Peter dropped in a line, they caught one. Soon their basket was filled with fish.

Suddenly, the quiet was broken by Caro's shrill yelps of pain. "What's happened to Caro?" Kirsten cried. The pup dashed from the woods.

He trembled all over, his tail between his legs. Still howling, he skidded to a stop on the bank and scuffed at his nose with both paws.

Kirsten and Peter splashed over to Caro. Peter dropped his pole and grabbed the frightened pup. "Kirsten, look at his nose!"

"He's been stung by a bee! Poor Caro! Hold him tightly, Peter!" Kirsten said.

Peter wrestled Caro still, then held the pup's head in both hands while Kirsten pulled out the stinger. "Poor puppy, poor puppy!" she whispered over and over against Caro's soft black ear. "I know it hurts, but I can make it better."

"I was going to take care of him, really I was!" Peter said. He looked as though he might cry. "But I was so busy catching fish, I didn't even notice when he wandered away."

"Don't worry, Caro will get over the sting," Kirsten said. She scratched the pup's chest as he licked and licked his nose. As she comforted him, she peered over his head at the deep woods where he'd wandered. The breeze smelled sweet, like blossoms. And in the distance, Kirsten thought she heard a faint hum, like the cat purring or Papa's

*"He's been stung by a bee! Poor Caro!*
*Hold him tightly, Peter!" Kirsten said.*

243

snore or maybe—bees. "I bet Caro found a bee tree," she said softly.

"A *bee* tree?" Peter said. "What's a bee tree?"

"A bee tree is one with a hole in it, where bees live. Listen!" Kirsten said.

Peter cocked his head the way Caro did when he heard a whistle. "I do hear something humming," he said after a moment.

"I think those are the bees!" Kirsten said. "And do you smell that sweet scent? It's basswood blossoms. Papa told me that bees love the blossoms on a basswood tree!"

"I smell blossoms," Peter said. "And I hear bees. But why are you so happy about a tree full of bees?" He rubbed his freckled cheek against Caro's ear. "A bee *stung* Caro."

Kirsten jumped to her feet and brushed the sand from her skirt. "Bees make *honey!*" she said. "A bee tree will be packed full of honeycombs."

Peter took Caro in his arms and cradled him. "What will we do with a tree full of honeycombs?" he asked.

"We'll get them out of the tree and bring them

to Mama. She'll use the honey to make cakes and cookies!" Kirsten said.

"Cookies!" Peter grinned.

"A bee tree is good for more than just cookies, though." Kirsten tried to talk calmly, but as she thought about a bee tree she grew more and more excited. "Finding a bee tree is like finding a treasure. There's so much honey in a bee tree, Papa will be able to sell some of it at Mr. Berkhoff's store. Then Papa can buy the things we need this summer. I heard him say he doesn't have enough money for a saw and the cloth Mama needs and boots for Lars, too. If we bring Papa a whole tree full of honey-combs, he won't have to worry about money. I bet he'll be able to buy everything!"

Now Peter was on his feet, too. "Everything we need? Then let's get the honey, Kirsten!"

Kirsten pressed her finger to her lips and peered at the woods. "We can't just *get* honey. First we have to find the bee tree."

"It must be nearby. Caro got stung, and we both hear buzzing," Peter said softly, as though the bee tree was his idea to begin with. "Listen again."

She listened. Yes, humming came from deep

in the woods. "If we could find a bee tree, we'd make Mama and Papa so proud," she whispered.

"Let's go look for the bee tree!" Peter's blue eyes were wide with excitement.

Kirsten rolled down the hems of her pantalettes and untucked her skirt. "We can't both go look. One of us has to stay here with Caro so he won't follow along and get stung again. You said you'd take care of him."

Peter's mouth turned down as he petted the shivering pup. "If you find a bee tree, *you* might get stung, too. Mama told us to be careful."

"Oh, I'll be careful! I'm just going to look. Wait right here for me, and don't let anything else happen to Caro!"

Kirsten turned to the shadowy woods. She ran a little way, then she walked. Every few steps she paused, stood very still, and listened. At first the hum of the bees was fainter. She turned around and went the other way. Now the hum was louder and the scent of blossoms was stronger. She stopped again. Yes, buzzing and a sweet smell came from over there! She made her way slowly down the hillside through the thorny raspberry bramble. At the

bottom of the hill was a sunny clearing circled
by a ring of trees. Across the clearing stood a
basswood tree, its cream-colored blossoms loud
with bees.

Kirsten crept closer. As she watched, a line
of bees flew back and forth between the blossoms
and a dead tree nearby. "The bee tree!" she said
softly. She could hardly believe her luck.

The bee tree had a tall trunk
with a jagged top. It was hollow,
with a small opening just above
Kirsten's head. Bees flew in and
out of the opening. There were so
many of them, thousands and
thousands! They must be filling
the whole tree with their honey!

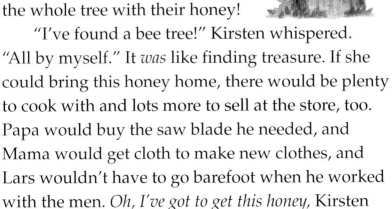

"I've found a bee tree!" Kirsten whispered.
"All by myself." It *was* like finding treasure. If she
could bring this honey home, there would be plenty
to cook with and lots more to sell at the store, too.
Papa would buy the saw blade he needed, and
Mama would get cloth to make new clothes, and
Lars wouldn't have to go barefoot when he worked
with the men. *Oh, I've got to get this honey*, Kirsten

said to herself. *There has to be a way, and I know I can find it.*

She carefully studied the bee tree. The opening was too high for her to reach unless she stood on a log. Maybe she'd have to climb a little, too. She saw that deep gashes scarred the trunk below the opening. Someone else had tried to climb the tree already. Someone else was after *her* honey!

Now Kirsten saw pawprints in the sand of the clearing. Bear pawprints! Bears were after her honey.

Kirsten backed slowly away from the bee tree and looked into the bushes. Papa and Mama had warned her many times to stay away from bears. But there was no sign of bears on this sunny morning. Probably the bears had gone away to another part of the woods and wouldn't come back. Anyway, this honey was hers, not the bears'. She had discovered it, and all she had to do now was figure out how to take it home.

She tried to think how Papa got honey from his beehives back in Sweden. She remembered he had used smoke to calm the bees, and he'd worn a veil to protect his head. Papa had packed his bee

*Someone else had tried to climb the tree already.*
*Someone else was after **her** honey!*

veil in the big trunk with the rest of the things they'd brought to America. Probably the bee veil would be in the barn. *If I use smoke and the bee veil, I could get this honey all by myself,* Kirsten thought.

With a sharp stone she scratched "K" on a birch tree at the edge of the clearing. Under her initial, she scratched, "B tree." Now the tree belonged to her and no one else could claim it. She ran back to where Peter waited for her.

"Peter, Peter, I was right!" she called as she ran to the stream. "There *is* a bee tree!"

Peter sat cross-legged, the pup in his lap. A frog hopped into the water as Kirsten scooted onto the bank beside him. "Are you sure it's a bee tree?" he said.

"Of course I'm sure! It's a hollow tree packed full of bees! Oh, Peter, it's so big there must be gallons of honey! Enough honey for cooking and trading, too. We could get the honey, we could take it home, we—"

"We could be stung just like Caro! Or worse!"
Peter said. He frowned up at Kirsten. "If we fool
with bees, we're asking for trouble. Let's tell Papa
about the tree. He can get the honey."

"No, no! I can get it myself. I found the bee tree
myself, didn't I?" She shoved her hands into her
waist the way Mama did when she wanted strict
attention. "Peter, are you afraid?"

Peter looked down at Caro. "I'm a little bit
afraid," he said. "I bet you are, too."

"I am not afraid! I'm braver than you are,"
Kirsten boasted.

"Mama says that sometimes brave is another
word for foolish," Peter said.

Kirsten grasped his shoulders. "Listen, I'm not a
bit foolish! I *know* I can get that honey. If you don't
want to help me, at least promise to keep the secret
while I make a plan." She looked right into his blue
eyes. "If you won't tell about the bee tree, I won't say
you didn't take care of Caro."

Peter squinched up his mouth, but after a
moment he nodded.

"Say *yes* out loud if you promise," Kirsten
insisted.

"Yes," he whispered.

"Good! Oh, Peter, everyone is going to be so proud of me!"

C H A P T E R
T W O

# IN THE
# BERRY PATCH

 "I love raspberry jelly!" Anna said. "I
love raspberry jelly even more than
I love maple syrup!"

"And your mama makes the very best jelly,"
Kirsten said. She and Peter were in the berry bramble
near the woods, helping their cousins Anna and
Lisbeth pick raspberries. Mama and Aunt Inger
needed berries to make preserves today.

Peter's and Anna's mouths were red with
raspberry juice because they ate almost as many
berries as they put into their pails. Kirsten couldn't
resist eating a small, plump berry now and then,
either. She thought the berry juice was as sweet as
honey. Everything made her think about honey

253

and the bee tree these days.

"Our mama is going to sell her jelly and jam to Mr. Berkhoff," Lisbeth said. "And Anna and I are going to help her make berry pies to eat when we go to town for the Fourth of July." She smiled at Kirsten from under the shade of her straw hat. Little dots of sun filtered through the brim and scattered across her nose like freckles.

"What's the Fourth of July?" Kirsten asked. Her own cloth sunbonnet was heavy with sweat. Picking berries was hot work!

"The Fourth of July is the day the Declaration of Independence was signed. Do you remember when Miss Winston read the Declaration of Independence aloud in school?" Lisbeth put one hand over her heart the way Miss Winston did when she recited with feeling. "'Life, liberty, and the pursuit of happiness!'" she said. "I love that part!"

"Will we all go to town on the Fourth of July?" Kirsten asked.

Anna set her bucket down and wiped her chin with her apron. "Oh, yes! Everyone goes to town on the Fourth of July. The whole day is

254

simply grand! There's a big parade with trumpets and drums. After the parade, there are speeches and music and a picnic, and contests and games, too."

Peter's face lit up. "Games? What kind of games?"

"Last year there was a three-legged race and a hurdle race," Anna said. "And a race to climb a greased pole. The prize was a whole dollar!" She pushed her straw hat back from her face. "The boys like the horse races, but I like the fireworks the very best."

"All day long guns and cannons boom and boom," Lisbeth said. "I don't like that so well."

"I'd love to hear the cannons!" Peter said. "Wa-boom! Wa-boom!" He made a fierce face that showed his berry-stained teeth. "And maybe I could win a running race."

Lisbeth looked doubtful. "Big boys run in those races, Peter. They'll run faster than you."

"But you could practice to run faster, Peter!" Anna said. "There are five more days until the Fourth." She held up five red-stained fingers.

Kirsten hadn't been thinking about the games and races. "Did you say people sell things in town on the Fourth of July?" she asked Lisbeth.

"Yes," Lisbeth said. "Everybody brings something to trade or sell. Last year we took sausages and spring chickens and butter, and preserves, too. Mama got a whole bolt of cloth, and there was even money left over. That's how Anna and I got our straw hats."

Kirsten's mind was back on the bee tree and the honey. She thought the Fourth of July would be the perfect time to sell honey in town. Maybe while everyone was busy picking berries, she could slip away into the woods for another look at her bee tree. If she was going to have that honey in five days, she'd have to work quickly.

Just beyond the raspberry patch were the deep woods where the bee tree was hidden. Kirsten moved along the berry bushes until she found a small opening she thought she could crawl through. No one saw her. They were still chattering about the fun on the Fourth of July.

Kirsten set down her berry bucket, got onto her hands and knees, and began to crawl through the bushes. Thorns pricked at her sleeves. She ducked lower until her elbows were on the ground. Her skirt rustled the leaves as she crept along.

Suddenly, right beside her, there was a loud snuffle. Alarmed, she stopped crawling. The snuffle came again, louder. When she turned, she looked right into the face of a black bear cub.

For a moment Kirsten couldn't get her breath. This was the first bear she'd seen up close. Papa had pointed out where bears slept through the winter. She'd seen bear tracks. But this round, furry thing was a *real* bear.

The cub stared at her from small, black-button eyes as it munched raspberries. As Kirsten stared back, the cub batted at a branch with its fat paw. Bits of leaves were caught in its thick fur. Kirsten felt herself smiling. The baby bear looked almost like a big puppy. She decided she had nothing to be afraid of. She thought it was even a good thing that the bear cub was up here in the berries, not over in the woods trying to raid the honey in her bee tree!

Then something startled the cub. It padded clumsily out of the berry patch and into the woods. A moment later, Kirsten saw Lisbeth thrashing through the bushes.

"Kirsten? Where are you? You wandered off."

"I'm right here," Kirsten called. She had to think of something to say so Lisbeth would stay where she was and not get any closer to the bee tree. "I thought the berries would be thicker here, but they're not."

As Kirsten moved toward Lisbeth, her foot hit her berry bucket. It tipped, and the berries spilled. She sat back on her heels to collect the spilled berries. "I just saw a bear cub. I think your footsteps frightened it away."

Lisbeth's mouth dropped open. "You saw *what?*"

"A little black bear cub," Kirsten said.

"Where did you see it?" Lisbeth said.

"It was right here in the bushes." Kirsten gathered a double handful of the spilled berries.

"Leave the berries, Kirsten!" Lisbeth whispered. "If there's a cub, the mother bear is sure to be nearby. She might come after us!" Lisbeth picked up Kirsten's empty bucket. "Let's go!" she hissed. "We have to get out of here!"

"Don't worry, Lisbeth. The cub was alone. It was cute," Kirsten said.

Lisbeth took Kirsten's wrist. "Cubs look cute, but bears are wild animals, Kirsten! Stay far, far away from them. They won't bother us if we don't bother them."

"But I wasn't bothering the cub. We just looked at each other," Kirsten said. "Anyway, it's gone now."

"But I'm sure it went back to its mother, and mother bears are dangerous when they're taking care of their cubs! The mother bear would chase us if she thought we'd harm her baby. If she caught us, she'd use her teeth and her claws. Come on, we'll look for berries somewhere else!"

Lisbeth was almost thirteen, the oldest of the children. Kirsten knew she couldn't ignore what Lisbeth told her. She got to her feet and followed her cousin to a different part of the woods. As they walked, Kirsten said to herself, *Nothing will keep me from getting my honey, not even bears!* Still, she was glad the only bear she'd seen near the bee tree was a little bear.

# BEARS!

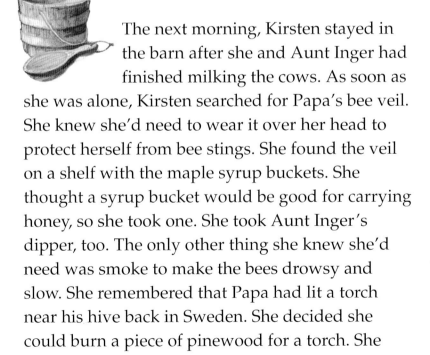

The next morning, Kirsten stayed in the barn after she and Aunt Inger had finished milking the cows. As soon as she was alone, Kirsten searched for Papa's bee veil. She knew she'd need to wear it over her head to protect herself from bee stings. She found the veil on a shelf with the maple syrup buckets. She thought a syrup bucket would be good for carrying honey, so she took one. She took Aunt Inger's dipper, too. The only other thing she knew she'd need was smoke to make the bees drowsy and slow. She remembered that Papa had lit a torch near his hive back in Sweden. She decided she could burn a piece of pinewood for a torch. She would ask Peter to hold it.

Kirsten hid her supplies behind the barn and went to find Peter. He was down at the stream getting water for Mama. "Peter, you've got to help me!" Kirsten called.

"Help you do what?" he said.

"Help me get the honey from the bee tree. I've got everything we need to do it today."

Peter waded out of the stream with the full bucket. "Did Papa say we could?"

"I didn't ask Papa. I want it to be a surprise. I want to surprise everyone. Think of what Mama will say when we bring home a whole bucket full of honey!"

"*I'm* thinking of what Papa will say if you get hurt," Peter said.

"I won't get hurt! I know just what to do. And if you help me, I'll give you some of the honey for your very own. I bet you could sell it at Mr. Berkhoff's store and get that little knife you saw there. Then you could whittle just like Lars does."

"I'd like that little knife," Peter said slowly. But still he looked worried.

"Take the water to Mama, then meet me behind the barn," Kirsten said. "Don't let anyone see you." She ran off before he had a chance to argue.

After what seemed a long time, Peter came to where Kirsten waited. She took his hand and squeezed it hard. "Good for you, Peter!" she said. "I knew you'd be brave enough to come with me! Here, take the dipper."

Right behind Peter came Caro. The pup jumped against Kirsten's legs. "Go home, Caro!" Kirsten whispered. "Shoo!" But Caro wouldn't go home. He licked Kirsten's hands and barked with excitement, as if he were in on the secret.

"He wants to come with us. Can't he help, too?" Peter asked.

"Well, I suppose he could stand guard for us. If bears come near the bee tree, Caro can chase them away," Kirsten said.

"*Bears?*" asked Peter.

"I just mean there are bears in the woods, and bears like honey, that's all," Kirsten said quickly. "There's nothing to be scared about. Let's go!"

Kirsten led the way into the forest. She and Peter

and the pup climbed a steep hill, then went down the other side. Soon they could hear the sound of the bee tree. "Listen to that hum, Peter! We're almost there," Kirsten said.

When Peter saw the bee tree and heard its loud hum, his eyes went wide. "I didn't know there were so many bees in the whole world!" he said. Caro dashed around the clearing. He sniffed the ground, but being stung had taught him not to go anywhere near the bees.

Kirsten set the bucket by her feet and picked up a pinewood stick for a torch. "You'll hold the torch right by the hive to keep the bees quiet while I dip out the honey," she told Peter. "But first I have to put on the bee veil."

"Can I get under the veil with you?" he asked in a small voice.

"You can stand under the veil if you keep one hand out to hold the torch. Roll down your shirt sleeves, Peter."

As Peter started to roll down his sleeves, Caro began to bark fiercely. Nearby, twigs cracked as something moved in the bushes. Caro ran toward the noise, yipping. Then the bear cub tumbled out of the thicket, with Caro right behind!

"Oh, no!" Kirsten cried. She dropped the bee veil in alarm. She hoped the cub was alone again. She hoped its mother wasn't near, because if a mother bear saw Caro chasing her cub, there would be trouble. The bear would think her cub was in danger and come after them all. Kirsten shook her apron and called to Caro. "Caro, stop it! Stop! Leave the cub alone!"

Caro turned to face the cub and bared his teeth. The cub growled back. Caro snapped and the cub showed its sharp teeth. They were going to fight!

"We've got to get Caro, Peter!" Kirsten cried. "Quick, quick!"

"Come, Caro!" Peter yelled. He picked up a stone and threw it at the cub. "And you, bear, you scat!"

Just then a deep growl echoed through the forest. Something huge broke from the shadows. The mother bear rushed to protect her cub! She lumbered swiftly forward, her head swinging. She

*Just then a deep growl echoed through the forest.*
*Something huge broke from the shadows.*

snorted at Caro, then flipped the pup away from her cub with a swift blow of her shaggy paw.

Caro yelped in pain as he landed in a pile of leaves. Then he was on his feet, streaking back home the way they'd come.

The bear turned to lick her cub, and Kirsten realized she and Peter had just this one chance to get away. She grabbed Peter's hand. "Quick! Climb that tree!"

They raced to the far side of the clearing. Kirsten made a step for Peter with her clasped hands. He jumped into it and stretched for the lowest branch of a big oak. He caught it, and Kirsten boosted him until he got a good grip. Peter dangled a moment, she shoved, and he threw his leg over and scrambled up onto the branch.

"Climb fast!" Kirsten cried. "Don't stop!"

"You come too!" Peter said. "Here's my hand!"

She grasped his hand and the branch and struggled up after him. Bits of bark showered into her face as they climbed higher up the tree.

The mother bear nuzzled her cub. Then she stepped in front of it and looked around the clearing again. Kirsten's ears hummed like the bees in the

KIRSTEN SAVES THE DAY

bee tree. Everyone knew black bears climbed trees easily. The bear could come right up this tree after them!

Again and again the mother bear shook her head, growling and snorting. Then she charged toward the tree, her paws slapping the ground like drumbeats. She stopped about ten feet away and peered up into the branches where Kirsten and Peter hung on.

"Dear God, please make the bear go away," Peter prayed. His eyes were tightly closed.

But Kirsten couldn't take her gaze from the bear. She could see the sharp teeth and long claws. It was so close she could smell the musky stink of its fur. If the bear came up the tree, she and Peter wouldn't have a chance.

Slowly, still watching the tree, the mother bear rose up on her hind legs. Her thick fur hung like a black robe as she sniffed the air. Then she lowered herself down onto all fours again and began to back up toward her cub.

When she reached the cub, the big bear gave it a swat as if to say, "Mind your mother!" The cub scuffled into the woods and its mother followed, looking back once over her heavy shoulder. The branches closed behind them, and they were gone.

Kirsten let her breath out very, very slowly. "Peter?"

"Are we still alive?" he whispered.

"The bear went away," Kirsten said. "Open your eyes."

Peter squinted two thin slits of blue. "Will it come back?"

"I don't know," Kirsten said softly. She got a better grip on the branch she held.

"I'm afraid to climb down," Peter said.

"Me too." Kirsten tried to swallow, but her mouth was too dry.

"Oh, Kirsten, the bear hurt Caro!"

"Caro could still run. He'll be all right. Don't cry," Kirsten said. But she felt tears on her own cheeks. She bit her lips and looked down at the claw marks in the dirt below them, then at the deep scratches around the bee tree. What if the bear came back? Oh, why had she decided to come here with no one but Peter? Why did she think she could get the honey herself? Why hadn't she been more careful?

Kirsten and Peter were still clutching the highest branch of the oak tree they'd climbed when they heard someone shouting in the distance, "Kirsten! Peter! Where are you?"

"It's Papa!" Peter cried.

"Here!" Kirsten called back to him. "We're here, Papa!" She remembered the whistle she wore around her neck and blew three short blasts.

Papa called again. His voice was closer now. Then he strode into the clearing, carrying his big rifle.

Peter began to skid and slide down the tree to him, but Kirsten stayed back. "Watch out, Papa!" she cried. "A bear chased us! It might be close by." She looked down through the leaves at Papa's red face.

Papa set his rifle against the tree. "I've got my gun. But no bear would come near this noise. They want to keep away from us as much as we do from them. You two come down here!"

Peter jumped from the lowest branch into Papa's arms, but Kirsten was almost as afraid of

Papa as she had been of the bear. Papa sounded very angry.

"Are you all right?" he asked Peter.

Peter nodded.

"Kirsten, are you all right?"

"Yes, Papa," she said.

"How did you find us?" Peter said. He held on to Papa's neck.

"The pup came home with his leg bleeding," Papa said. "It looked like a bear had clawed him. I know he likes to tag along with you, and I was afraid you'd met up with bears. So I grabbed my

271

gun and followed the trail of his blood back through the woods. Then I heard your shouts and the whistle." He set Peter on the ground and held his arms up to Kirsten.

She jumped down, her face hot. Papa set her on the ground and took her shoulder in his strong grip. "Tell me what you're doing here," he said sternly. When Papa was angry, his eyes seemed to burn like the fire in the cookstove.

Kirsten kept her gaze on her dusty feet. "I found that bee tree, Papa," she said.

He glanced at it for the first time. "Well, that's a good find. Go on."

"It's full of honey," Kirsten said. "Peter and I wanted to get the honey for you. We thought you could sell it at the store." She tried to smile, but her lips felt numb.

"And you went to get it by yourselves?" Papa asked.

"Kirsten said she knew what to do, and that we could surprise you!" Peter said.

"You agreed, Peter. You said yes!" Kirsten hissed.

"Then Caro chased a cub, and the big bear

came," Peter hurried on.

Papa stroked his beard. There were deep furrows in his brow, like the ones his plow made in the field. "Did you know bears came to the bee tree, Kirsten?"

"I saw a bear once, but only a baby," she murmured.

"But you know mother bears are always near their cubs to protect them! You did a very, very foolish thing! You put your life and Peter's life in danger! You've got to be careful in the woods!" Papa's voice boomed.

Peter pushed between Papa and Kirsten. "But Kirsten saved my life! When the big bear came, she helped me up in the tree so I'd be safe! She was very brave!"

Papa took Peter's hand, then Kirsten's. "Listen to me! It isn't brave to go near bears, it's dangerous! The only way to be safe from bears is to stay away from them. And never, never go near the cubs, do you hear me?"

"I'm sorry, Papa." Kirsten could hardly hear her own voice.

"We thought you'd be happy about a bee tree," Peter whispered.

"We thought that if we brought you the honey, you'd be able to get all the things you need at Mr. Berkhoff's store," Kirsten added.

"The honey in this tree will be valuable, I'm sure of that," Papa said. "But the bees are an even better find." Papa looked stern. "If you had broken into the hive with that dipper, you would have destroyed the colony of bees. You might have ruined the honey, too. And what's much worse, you'd have been badly stung! Kirsten, you're ten years old! You're old enough to take good care of yourself and your little brother. You're old enough to know better!"

Kirsten was ashamed. Because of her reck-lessness she'd put Peter in danger. The pup had been clawed. Mama and Papa were frightened and upset. And she had almost destroyed the treasure she'd found. She couldn't keep tears from rolling down her cheeks. "Oh, Papa, I'm so sorry! Truly I am!"

Papa leaned down and looked into her eyes. "I can see I don't need to paddle you. You've been punished enough. Come home now." He picked up the bee veil and the syrup bucket, then his rifle. "I'll come back tomorrow and take the honey *and* the bees to the farm."

# BRINGING BACK
# THE BEES

"Do you have the saw?" Papa asked Lars.

"Yes, I have it," Lars said. He lifted the big saw onto his shoulder.

Kirsten and Peter watched from where they sat in the barn loft. Today Papa and Lars were going to saw down the bee tree and move the colony of bees back to the farm. A round straw skep would be the bees' new home. Papa and Lars would set it in the meadow near the barn, and the bees would fill the skep with honeycombs. By fall, Papa would be able to harvest more honey.

"Why are we taking the bellows?" Lars asked.

"Smoke will calm the bees before we move

them," Papa said. "We need the bellows to blow the smoke inside the bee tree."

"See, our torch wouldn't have worked anyway," Peter whispered to Kirsten.

She didn't answer him. She had her chin in her hands, and she was thinking. When she shut her eyes, she remembered the bear rushing at the tree where she and Peter hid. She didn't like to have these bad memories. "I should go back to the clearing where the bear chased us," she said very softly.

Peter sat on his heels and stared at her. "Why do you want to go back? It was terrible to be chased!" He put his hand on her forehead the way Mama did when they were sick. "Do you have a fever?"

"No, I don't have a fever. But I dreamed about bears last night," Kirsten said. "I think if I don't go back to the woods today, I won't ever have the nerve to go again."

"Well, I'm not going, not even with Papa and Lars," Peter said firmly.

When Papa picked up the bee veils, Kirsten climbed down the ladder. "I can carry those for you,

Papa," she said. "You have to carry the skep."

Papa raised his eyebrows. "Are you asking to come with me and Lars?"

Kirsten nodded. She thought Papa was still angry at her, because she hadn't seen him smile since he had found her and Peter in the tree yesterday. "Could I come with you, please?"

Lars scratched his blond head. "Aren't you afraid of the bears, Kirsten?"

Lars was fifteen, and it seemed to Kirsten that he wasn't afraid of anything in the world. "Yes, I'm afraid," she said. She could barely hear her own voice. "But I think I'll be less afraid if I go back with you and Papa."

Lars grinned at her. But Papa said sternly, "Moving bees isn't play, Kirsten."

"I know, Papa," she said.

"If you come with us, will you do exactly as I tell you?" Papa asked.

"I will. I'll do exactly as you tell me." Kirsten grabbed the bee veils. She glanced up at Peter, who sat at the top of the ladder with his arms around his knees.

"Could Peter come, too?" she asked Papa.

Before Papa could answer, Peter said, "I'm going to stay home and look after Caro!"

Papa took the straw skep in his arms. "Peter, tell your mother that Kirsten is going with me and Lars. Mama's not to worry. Kirsten will be safe with us."

Peter slid down the ladder and ran to the house. Kirsten followed Papa and Lars back to the woods.

At the clearing, Papa took Kirsten's hand and led her to a spot across the open space from the bee tree. He drew a mark on the ground with the toe of his boot. "Stay right here, Kirsten. Don't come even a single step closer to the bee tree," Papa said.

Kirsten stood right on the mark Papa had drawn. Sunlight slanted through the trees, and the air smelled of basswood blossoms. But even on this pretty morning it was easy to remember the mother bear snorting and pawing here. Kirsten watched Papa and Lars closely, so that she wouldn't think too much about the bear.

They put the veils over their hats and pulled them down to cover their faces. Then Papa started a fire by the bee tree. When the fire was going, Lars used the bellows to pump smoke inside the hole. Big puffs of black smoke disappeared into the hollow of the bee tree. At first the bees buzzed more loudly. Then they were quieter, as though they might have fallen asleep.

"Now," Papa said to Lars, "we'll saw off the top of the tree."

They each took an end of the saw and began to cut the dead tree just above the place where the bees lived. Soon the tree top crashed into the clearing. Kirsten looked over her shoulder. If any bears were near, that thud would scare them away.

Quickly, Papa put the straw skep over the part of the tree that was still standing. He thumped the tree to move the bees up into the skep. When he thought that all the bees were inside, he lifted the skep onto a long board. Then he and Lars took the saw again. They cut a thick log from the stump. It was filled with combs of honey. They loaded the log full of honey onto the board, too, and each picked up an end.

"Let's head for home," Papa said.

As they left the clearing, Kirsten looked around

*Quickly, Papa put the straw skep*
*over the part of the tree that was still standing.*

281

one last time. She wasn't so frightened now. She knew there were bears in the forest and that they would always be here. But she knew, too, that she could be wise and careful. If she didn't bother them, the bears would stay away. She ran to catch up with Papa and Lars.

When they got back to the farm, Papa and Lars put the bee skep on a platform in the meadow. Then they carried the log full of honey back to the cabin. Mama was waiting there with hot water to melt the waxy honeycombs. Peter was scrubbing out crocks to fill with honey.

Kirsten stood a little way away, watching.

"Is it a big colony of bees?" Mama asked Papa.

"It's a good, big one!" Papa said. "It will make lots more honey. And look at all the honey in this log now. Even if we keep enough for cooking, there will be plenty to sell in town on Tuesday."

Mama clasped her hands in pleasure. Kirsten could see that Mama was happy. Still, that didn't make Kirsten feel as proud about the honey as she'd expected to be.

As though she read Kirsten's mind, Mama

turned to her. "Why are you looking so sad, dear?" Mama said.

"I thought *I* could get the honey for you," Kirsten blurted out. "I thought I could do it myself. I wanted to help you get the things we need from Mr. Berkhoff's store. But instead of helping . . ." Suddenly she couldn't talk anymore. Her eyes blurred with tears. She had nothing to be proud of after all. It had taken Papa and Lars to get the honey. All she'd done was to put herself and Peter in danger. And Caro had been clawed. Tears dripped off her face onto her dress.

Mama's arm went around Kirsten's shoulders. "I'm proud of you for finding the bee tree. Papa and I know you wanted to help. And you *did* help. You found us good honey to use this summer, and enough to sell in town, too. And since your papa brought the bees home, we can count on having more honey next fall. All because of you, Kirsten." Mama gave her a squeeze. "Now we have work to do to get this honey ready to sell on the Fourth of July. We're going to need your help again."

Kirsten blinked at Mama through her tears. She wanted to be just like Mama when she grew up.

"You're a smart girl, Kirsten," Papa said. He wiped tears from her chin with his thumb. "And you're certainly brave. Nothing seems to scare you. You just have to remember to be brave *and* careful at the same time." Papa's smile told her everything was all right.

CHAPTER
FIVE
—

# THE BEST
# BASSWOOD HONEY

"Get your sunbonnet, Kirsten!" Anna called. "The wagon's hitched! It's time to go to town!"

Kirsten emptied the dishwater on the garden behind the little cabin. She wiped her hands, grabbed her sunbonnet, and hurried out to the wagon. It was loaded with crates of chickens, baskets filled with sausages, jars of jelly, and two big crocks of Kirsten's honey. Papa, Lars, and Uncle Olav were squeezed into the front seat. Mama and Aunt Inger were on chairs behind them. Mama held the baby in her arms.

Kirsten scrambled up onto the very back of the wagon, beside Peter. They sat with their feet dangling over the back board, crowded in beside the big picnic hampers. As the wagon rolled down the road, crows swooped overhead and dust billowed behind the wheels. From behind the wagon came a high-pitched yip yip yip.

"Caro's chasing the wagon!" Peter cried.

"Papa, please stop!" Kirsten called.

Papa reined in the horses. Caro appeared out of the dust, his pink tongue lolling. He jumped against the wagon wheel and wagged his tail.

"Even with his hurt leg he chased us!" Peter said. He climbed down and petted the pup.

"He must want to go with us very badly," Kirsten said. "Could we take him along, Papa?"

"There will be a lot of dogs in town today," Papa said. "Caro might get in a dog fight. He'll be better off on the farm, Kirsten."

"But I'll tie a piece of rope around his neck and keep him close to us," Kirsten begged.

"We'll take good care of him!" Peter chimed in.

"I suppose that two children should be able to manage one puppy," Papa said. "Bring him up in the wagon, Peter. Let's get going."

Caro settled on Kirsten's lap. "We'll look after

you, I promise," she whispered against his silky ear.

Soon the Larsons' wagon was joined by many other wagons on the road to Maryville. Everyone shouted and laughed and waved to each other through the dust.

"Isn't the Fourth of July grand?" Anna cried. "It's almost like Christmas in the summer!"

"I can already hear the guns and cannons in town!" Peter said.

The streets of Maryville were crowded with wagons and buggies. People filled the lanes and the little park in the center of town. Papa found a place near Mr. Berkhoff's store to unhitch the horses. Everyone climbed off the wagon. Then Papa, Uncle Olav, and Lars began to unpack the boxes and crates.

Before they finished, Mr. Berkhoff came out of his store. He wiped his hands on his apron as he looked over the goods the Larsons had to sell him. "What have you got for me?" he said. "More of your good sausages, I see."

"And raspberry preserves and maple syrup, too!" Aunt Inger stepped forward to show off what they had brought. She was good at making a bargain.

Mr. Berkhoff bent down to peer into the crates of chickens. "More hens? I'm not sure I can take more hens. Everyone seems to have brought them to market today."

"Not as plump as these hens," Aunt Inger said quickly. She stood right by Mr. Berkhoff's side. "We raise the plumpest chickens! And take a look at the wheels of cheese. You don't see cheese like ours every day. It's surely worth a lot." She smiled confidently.

But Mr. Berkhoff scratched the bald spot on his head and frowned. "Well, that depends on what you folks will be wanting to buy."

"Cloth!" Mama and Aunt Inger spoke at the same time.

"But first we need boots for our Lars, and a saw blade and nails," Mama added.

Mr. Berkhoff glanced at Lars, who lifted baskets from the wagon. "That boy has grown a foot taller since I saw him last," he said. "I hope I've got boots big enough! Did you bring any more of your little wood carvings to sell, Lars? One of the town ladies asked about them."

Lars's cheeks turned red. He wasn't used to being praised. "I brought a few carvings," he said.

"Good!" Mr. Berkhoff said. But still he didn't smile as he looked over the stacks of boxes and crates. He seemed to be adding them up in his head.

Peter leaned against Kirsten's side. He whispered, "Shall I ask Mr. Berkhoff about the little knife, so I can learn to carve like Lars?"

Kirsten pinched Peter's arm. "Hush, Peter! We might not even have enough money for what we need. We won't be able to buy any extra things."

"But you *said,*" he murmured.
Then he pressed his lips together.
He knew as well as Kirsten did
that the important things like a
saw blade and boots came first.

Now Aunt Inger pushed forward the crate that held the boxes of beeswax and crocks of honey. "I've saved a surprise for last, Mr. Berkhoff!" she said with the same excited voice she used when she served her special cake for Sunday dinner.

*Kirsten pinched Peter's arm. "Hush, Peter!" she said.*
*"We might not even have enough money for what we need."*

Mr. Berkhoff's gray eyebrows went up as she handed him a box of the beeswax. "What's this? Beeswax!" he said.

"It's fine, clean wax, as you can see," Aunt Inger said.

A little smile pushed up the corners of Mr. Berkhoff's lips. "This beeswax will sell for candles and for furniture polish, too. The town is growing, you know. Some fine ladies who have time to polish their furniture are moving here."

Papa held up one of the crocks of honey. He pulled off the cork and offered the crock to Mr. Berkhoff. "And here's honey, too. Basswood honey. Why don't you have a taste?"

Mr. Berkhoff dipped his finger into the crock, licked the honey, and a grin spread across his red face. "Where did you get such fine honey, Mr. Larson?"

"Our Kirsten has a nose as good as a bear's for honey!" Papa said. "She found a bee tree in the forest, and we moved the hive to our farm." He pulled out his handkerchief and wiped his forehead. "What do you think of it?"

"Delicious!" said Mr. Berkhoff. He took another

taste and then another. "So Kirsten found this honey! You can bet I'll tell the folks who buy it where it came from. We don't often get such pure basswood honey." He smiled at Kirsten. "This will be worth something, young lady."

She wanted to smile back, but she was still too worried to feel happy. Even with the honey, maybe there wouldn't be enough to buy what they needed.

"You women go inside the store and look over my pretty new calico," Mr. Berkhoff said to Mama and Aunt Inger. "The men will finish up out here, and we'll settle our accounts."

Mama and Aunt Inger made their way through the crowd in front of the store. Anna and Lisbeth went right behind them. Kirsten and Peter tied Caro in the wagon where he'd be safe, then ran to catch up to the others.

As Kirsten stepped inside the door, she smelled the mouth-watering scents of spices and coffee and sausages. The little store hummed as loudly as a beehive with the voices of the shoppers. Mama and Aunt Inger joined the women who unrolled bolts of cloth on the wide counter. Anna bent over the candy display and Lisbeth looked at lace.

"I'm going to look at pocket knives," Peter said to Kirsten. "It won't hurt just to *look,* will it?"

She gave him a little shove toward the display of knives. "Pretend you can have any knife you choose," she said. "Pretending won't hurt."

Kirsten stopped by Lisbeth to run her finger along a length of pink ribbon. On the shelf above the spools of ribbons was a broad-brimmed straw sun hat like the one Lisbeth wore. Gently, Kirsten traced the wide brim of the new hat. *If I could have anything in the store, I'd pick this straw hat,* she thought. *It would be so cool and so pretty on these hot summer days.*

Papa's voice boomed from behind her. "Do you need two hats, Kirsten? Isn't your sunbonnet warm enough for you?"

Kirsten could tell he was teasing her, but she blushed just the same. She knew better than to ask for what they couldn't afford. "I was just pretending, Papa," she said. "It's lucky I don't need a straw hat, because I'm sure this one wouldn't fit me."

"Let's try it on and see," Papa said. He lifted the hat and held it above her while she pulled off her damp sunbonnet. When he set the straw hat on her head, it was as light as a breeze.

"You've earned a special treat today, Kirsten," Papa said. "I worried that we wouldn't have enough to sell for all the things we needed from Mr. Berkhoff. But when he saw that beeswax and tasted your honey, I knew we'd have enough and a little more besides. So you and Peter may each choose something for yourself."

"Peter, too?" Kirsten whispered. She was almost too happy to speak.

"He wants a knife," Papa said. "And you, Kirsten, would you like this straw hat?"

She nodded. Papa settled the hat on her head. Kirsten gazed in the looking glass and smiled at the blond girl in the straw hat who was smiling back. She saw Papa's face over her shoulder. Then, over her other shoulder, Kirsten watched Mama hand the baby to Aunt Inger and come to join them.

"What this hat needs is a nice ribbon and a little decoration," Mama said. She tied a length of black ribbon and a bunch of bright red cherries around it. Now there were three smiling faces in the looking glass.

Suddenly a ratatat of drums started up in the park. Fiddles joined the drums in a lively marching tune.

Peter ran outside. In a minute he was back in the open door of the store, with Caro on his rope right beside him. "It's the parade!" Peter shouted. "The parade is beginning right now! Come on, come on!"

Papa patted Kirsten on the shoulder. "Go on, wear your hat to the parade! A girl needs a straw hat on a day like this. I'll tell Mr. Berkhoff to add it to our account."

"Thank you, Papa!" Kirsten said. "Oh, thank you!"

"Take care that Peter doesn't get in the way of the horses," Mama told her. "Your Papa and I will be along in a moment."

Holding her hat on with one hand, Kirsten took Caro's rope from Peter. Caro's tail beat happily against her skirt as she and Peter hurried to join the crowd.

FOR MY MOTHER,
NADINA FOWLER

# 1854
# CHANGES FOR
# KIRSTEN

## *A Winter Story*

CHAPTER
ONE

# ON THE TRAP LINE

"Kirsten can't come with us!" John Stewart said. "Trapping is work for boys, not girls."

"Let her come along," Kirsten's brother Lars said. "Kirsten knows the forest. She knows the ways of the animals. She can help us out, John."

But John crossed his arms over his chest and shook his head. "Setting traps is dangerous. She could get hurt."

"She won't set traps," Lars said. "She'll help us decide *where* to set traps."

"Opening the traps and taking the animals out is dangerous, too!" John spoke as though Kirsten weren't standing right next to him.

301

"You and I will open the traps and get the animals out. After we skin them, Kirsten can help carry the pelts home," Lars said. "Just yesterday you said we should bring someone along to help us."

"And today I say she stays home with the women and children!" John said. "Trapping is hard enough without a girl to look after."

Kirsten bit her lip and looked down at her boots. The January snow came up almost to her knees. She wore all her flannel petticoats, her warmest skirt, and two pairs of wool socks, but still she trembled with cold. Her breath was a frost on her muffler. It would get colder yet as the afternoon went on. Winter in Minnesota was much harder than the winters in Sweden! But Kirsten wanted to go with Lars and John on the trap line. She was tired of working in the small, smoky cabin. And Lars was right—she did know about animals and the forest. She could help on the trap line, if only John would give her a chance.

"She knows how to spot the holes where beavers come through the ice," Lars said. "She knows the tracks raccoons make, and the tracks of muskrats and foxes. She can help us choose where to set traps for them. Don't be stubborn, John."

John peered down at Kirsten and frowned. "What will you do if we find a live beaver in a trap? It might bite you!"

"If we find a live beaver, I'll stay back," Kirsten said firmly. "Don't worry, I won't get bitten."

"Let her come with us this once," Lars said.

John huffed out a white breath. "All right. She can come this one time. But if she's trouble, she can't come again. Agreed, Kirsten?"

Kirsten looked him right in the eye. "Agreed," she said.

"Then let's go!" Lars said. "It's already afternoon, and we have a long, long way to walk before dark."

He swung his arms to get the warmth back into his hands, then strapped on his snowshoes. John and Kirsten strapped on snowshoes, too, and pulled their rucksacks onto their backs.

John was thirteen, but almost as tall as Lars. He had cheerful brown eyes and curly dark hair like his sister Mary. Mary was Kirsten's friend. Why wouldn't John be friends, too? Why was he so set against Kirsten going along on the trap line?

Lars picked up the rifle and followed John into the woods. Kirsten hugged herself for warmth, but she kept up with the boys' long strides.

They were going to check each of the traps the boys had set in the woods. If it was a good day, they would find dead animals in many of the traps. They'd skin the animals, dry the fur pelts, and sell the pelts at the general store.

The boys did this hard work because Papa, Uncle Olav, and John's father were gone for the winter. The men were working in a logging camp where they could make money cutting down trees. In the spring they would come back home. Until then, the women and children had to do all the winter farm work and make what money they could. Kirsten thought it was awful to have Papa gone. But she knew there was no other way her family could save money for a farm of their own.

As Kirsten walked, she studied the deer tracks that crossed the trail. She watched a red-tailed hawk circling overhead. She spied the bright red swoop of a cardinal. She was so happy to be out of the cabin and into the woods that she forgot how cold it was or how far she had walked with Lars and John.

They were in deep woods, far from the cabin, when Kirsten saw something strange—a birch tree bent over by a length of rope staked to the ground. "Lars, John, look!" she said.

The boys stopped. John didn't seem surprised to see the bent tree and the rope. "That's a snare trap for mink," he said.

"A trap made with rope?" Kirsten said. "All our traps are metal."

"We set metal traps because they're modern," John said. "But Old Jack still traps the old-fashioned way, with rope traps. That trap must be one of his."

"Who's Old Jack?" Kirsten asked.

John stamped back to the trail, and Kirsten hurried to keep up with him.

"Old Jack is the oldest trapper in these parts," John told her. "He came west as an explorer and stayed on. He lives by himself, way back in the woods. He doesn't have a family and never did."

*"That must be one of Old Jack's traps," John said.*
*"Old Jack still traps the old-fashioned way."*

"Old Jack dresses all in leather clothes, the old way," Lars added.

"Ohhhh," Kirsten said.

John grinned over his shoulder at her. "There's nothing to be scared of. Old Jack is different, but he's wise. Once he showed me where to set some traps for foxes. He likes to trap mink and martens and fishers—furs worth a lot of money."

"Well, I hope we don't meet up with Old Jack," Kirsten said. She peered into the purple shadows under the pines.

"If we did meet Old Jack, he'd give us a hand," John said. "But I doubt if we'll see him. He doesn't like to come where other folks are."

As John spoke, Kirsten saw a big jackrabbit jump from under a pine tree. Quickly, she pointed. Lars had the rifle at his shoulder. He took a shot, and the rabbit tumbled down. "Rabbit stew for supper tonight!" Lars said. He ran ahead to pick up the rabbit.

Kirsten thought of the delicious stew Mama made with carrots and onions and potatoes. Her stomach moaned with hunger, and she munched a piece of bread from her pocket. It would be a long time before they would be home for supper.

"Our traps begin in that ravine," Lars said. "Come on!"

In the first trap, they found a big raccoon. Lars quickly skinned it and put the skin in his rucksack.

In the second trap they found another. "We're having good luck today," John said as he skinned the raccoon.

"Maybe it's because Kirsten came along," Lars said. He winked at her.

"Maybe it's because we set our traps right," John said in his stubborn way. But Kirsten thought he almost smiled at her.

She tucked her hands under her armpits for warmth and looked up the hill into the oak trees. The sun was sinking low behind them. Many animals in the forest slept all day and woke up at dusk. At this time of day she might see a deer, Kirsten thought.

And as though she'd wished it here, a big buck stepped into the clearing! He appeared as silently as a shadow. Kirsten held her breath. Her heart was beating fast. The buck was so beautiful. But before Lars could reach for his rifle, the buck leaped away. They saw his white tail flash, and he was gone. Lars slapped his knee in disappointment. "If I'd shot him, there would have been meat for our family and yours, too, John!"

"We've got the rabbit," John said. "And we might find some muskrats in the water traps. They're good to eat, too. Let's go on."

It wasn't long before John, Lars, and Kirsten each had a rucksack full of pelts. It was growing dark when they came to the last trap. A small raccoon was in it. When Lars bent down to spring the trap, the raccoon opened its bright eyes and raised a paw.

"Look, just its tail is caught," John said. "It's not even bloody. I think the trap only bumped its head and knocked it out."

The young raccoon pawed at Lars's mitten but didn't even show its teeth.

"It's dazed, that's all," Lars said. "Anyway, it's too little to be worth anything. Let's let it go."

Kirsten knelt to look at the young raccoon. It made a noise like a kitten. Its pawprints in the snow looked like little hands. She knew a stunned raccoon wouldn't live long in the woods. A wolverine or a

badger would get it. "Let me take it home," she said.
"I can take care of it until it gets strong enough to
look after itself. Then I'll let it go."

Lars shook his head as though he couldn't
believe his ears. "You can't make a pet out of a wild
animal, Kirsten!"

"I won't make a pet of it. I'll just keep it until
it's healthy again," Kirsten said. "Remember how I
nursed the crow with the broken wing?"

"That was a bird," Lars said. "Raccoons are
different. You know how much trouble they cause
at the farm."

310

The little raccoon pawed at the tip of her snow-shoe. It *was* almost like a kitten, Kirsten thought. If she kept it in a box for a few days, it would be strong again.

John bent down and picked up the raccoon. It still didn't show its teeth. "I don't understand why it's so gentle," he said.

"It won't be gentle when it comes to its senses," Lars said. "Let it go, John."

But instead of letting the raccoon go, John handed it to Kirsten. "You do seem to know about animals, Kirsten. Maybe you can help this one."

His smile told her he was glad she'd come trapping with them. Although her lips were numb with cold, she smiled back at him.

She put the raccoon into her rucksack on top of the furs. "Come on, the moon is up already," she said. "Let's hurry home before we get caught in the dark." She wrapped her muffler over her nose and went ahead of the boys down the trail toward the little farm in the valley.

# FIRE!

After supper, Lars and John divided
the pelts into two equal piles. John
took his share home. Lars and Kirsten
took theirs to the barn. Kirsten found an empty nail
box, lined it with hay, and put the little raccoon
inside. It nestled down and closed its eyes. Then
Kirsten and Lars pulled the pelts over wooden
stretchers and scraped them with knives.

As she scraped the pelts, Kirsten watched the
raccoon sleep. It seemed tame already. She thought
there was no need to worry about it causing
trouble.

Soon Mama came to the barn to call them for
bed. Her eyes went wide when she saw the raccoon

in the box. "Children, why did you bring a raccoon home? You know how much mischief they cause!" she said. "Remember the raccoon that stole the fish for our supper right off the table?"

Lars looked up from his work. "This raccoon was knocked out by a trap. Kirsten brought it home so it can get on its feet again."

"Wild animals don't want to be touched," Mama said. "If it let you pick it up, maybe it's sick. Sick animals can be dangerous."

Kirsten covered the raccoon's box with a piece of wood. "It's not sick, Mama. It's just dazed and needs rest. When it's stronger, I'll let it go," she said softly. She thought of John's smile when he put the little raccoon into her hands—John wanted to be her friend.

Mama pulled her thick shawl over her head. Even in the barn it was shivering cold tonight. "I don't think your papa would want a wild animal in the barn. Be sure you keep it in the box, Kirsten."

Lars picked up the lantern and put his hand on Mama's shoulder. "Let's go back to the cabin, Mama. And don't worry. It's just a little raccoon. Kirsten will take care of it."

Mama sighed. "But you mustn't bring it near the cabin. And let it go the minute it seems well, do you promise?"

"I promise," Kirsten said quickly. She thought her mother looked very tired. Mama had so much work to do these days, and she missed Papa. They all missed Papa.

Before they left the barn, Kirsten put the raccoon's box under the hay where it was warmer. "Get well," she whispered to the sleeping raccoon. "Get well quickly!"

When Kirsten woke up the next morning, the first thing she thought of was the raccoon. But there wasn't time for her to go look at it. She had to feed baby Britta her oatmeal. And she had to make breakfast for everyone. Today was baking day, and Mama was already busy making dough for their bread.

"Kirsten, I'm going up to Aunt Inger's house to bake our bread in her big oven," Mama said. She picked up the tray of dough. "While I'm gone, I want you to wash out the diapers and help Peter learn his numbers and—"

"And look after Britta!" Kirsten finished for Mama.

Mama smiled. "That baby sister of yours does need a lot of looking after, doesn't she?"

"She crawls everywhere!" Peter said.

Britta pulled herself up on his knee and tugged at the slate he held. In her long flannel dress and many sweaters, Britta was as chubby as a bear cub. She *was* sweet, but she was a lot of trouble, too.

Peter raised the slate out of her reach. "I wish it wasn't too cold to have school," he said.

"I've never heard you wish for school before," Mama said.

"Britta can't come to school," Peter scowled.

Mama rumpled his yellow hair with her free hand. "I know it's hard to be cooped up in the cabin all winter. But soon it will be spring, and you'll be running outside again. While I'm gone you must shell the walnuts, Peter. When I come back, I'll make a little cake for supper. Be good children."

"Yes, Mama," Kirsten said as Mama went out the door. Kirsten wished she could go to Aunt Inger's house and play with her cousins Anna and

Lisbeth. She wished she could go on the trap line again today with Lars and John. But Mama needed her to stay in the cabin and work.

Kirsten chipped ice off the window and gazed at the barn. Was the little raccoon getting better? Was it warm enough in the box? Maybe she'd just take a quick peek at it before she did the washing.

"Peter, you hold Britta for a minute, will you? I'm going to run to the barn. When I get back, I'll tell you why."

Peter looked grumpy, but he held out his arms for the baby.

Without buttoning her sweater, Kirsten raced to the barn. She dug the raccoon's box out from under the hay and peeked under the board. Good! The raccoon's eyes were open. But the little thing trembled with cold. It missed its warm nest with the other raccoons. Kirsten decided that if she took the box to the cabin—just for a little while—the raccoon would warm up and get stronger more quickly. She tucked the box under her arm and ran back.

Kirsten set the box by the cookstove. "Come look, Peter!"

Peter put the baby down in the center of the bed and crouched beside Kirsten. She lifted the board. Peter peered in. "Kirsten, what a funny face it has! It looks so friendly!"

Before Kirsten could warn him not to, Peter scooped up the raccoon like a toy and set it on the floor.

Right away the raccoon dashed under the bed. "Catch it, Peter!" Kirsten said. Peter flopped onto his belly and grabbed for the scampering raccoon. But the frightened animal was much too quick for him. It darted across the floor under a chair.

"We have to catch it!" Kirsten snatched at the raccoon's striped tail. "It might break something!"

The raccoon raced up the chair and leaped onto the shelf by the cookstove. As it scurried across the shelf, it knocked a tin cup and a candlestick onto the floor.

Britta laughed out loud. She thought the chase was a new game. But Kirsten was alarmed. "Peter, get it back in the box!" she cried. Her fingers brushed the raccoon's paw. She almost had it!

Kirsten knew the raccoon wanted to get out of the cabin and back to the woods. Maybe she should open the door and let it run free. But before she could get to the door, the raccoon jumped on top of the table. Peter reached with both hands. The raccoon leaped and tipped over the oil lamp that sat on the table.

The lamp crashed to the floor and broke. Flames shot up from the spilled oil and caught the tablecloth.

"Oh, no! Oh, no!" Kirsten cried. She jerked the burning cloth from the table and stamped on it. But now the spilled oil spread. Suddenly the oil was a trail of fire across the floor!

How could she put out the fire? She dumped the wash water onto it, but that wasn't enough. The burning oil crept under the bed where Britta sat.

Kirsten grabbed the baby and pushed her into Peter's arms. "Run to Aunt Inger's, Peter! Tell everyone to come help! Tell them to bring water!"

She opened the door and shoved Peter on his way. The raccoon darted out right by his heels. "Hurry, Peter, hurry!" she called after him.

*"Run to Aunt Inger's, Peter!" Kirsten cried.*
*"Tell everyone to come help! Tell them to bring water!"*

Kirsten grabbed the coffeepot and splashed it on the fire under the bed, but that didn't help either. If only she had more water, a lot of water! Already flames had caught the blanket and the straw mattress. She beat at them with a rug. But quickly the fire spread up the cabin wall where the clothes hung. Moment by moment the fire grew stronger. Their cabin was burning down! What could she save?

She picked up the candlesticks Mama had brought from Sweden. Would Mama want her candlesticks most of all? Maybe the rifle was more important, or the stew pot. There wasn't time to think! Kirsten's eye caught the big blue trunk that had once held everything her family owned in America. The family Bible and their extra clothes were stored in the trunk. Surely it was the most important thing of all to save. She shoved the rifle and the candlesticks into the trunk and latched the lid.

But the trunk was so heavy! Kirsten could hardly budge it, and now the flames were climbing into the rafters over her head. Somehow she dragged the trunk to the door. Then she got behind it and shoved. The fire crackled at her back. Flames roared in the shingle roof overhead! Hurry, hurry! She put her shoulder to the trunk and pushed again.

As the trunk went through the door, Mama and Aunt Inger came running. "Mama, help me!" Kirsten cried.

"Kirsten, come here!" Mama grabbed Kirsten's hand and pulled her away from the burning cabin. Aunt Inger yanked the trunk away, too. Now Lisbeth and Anna and Peter came with buckets of water. They tossed the water at the fire. "More water!" Aunt Inger cried. She filled her apron with snow and pitched it at the fire. Lisbeth and Anna filled their buckets with snow to toss on the flames. Peter and Kirsten scooped snow with their hands and threw it. But the flames only leaped higher.

Fire filled the cabin and burst out the window and the door. The cabin burned like a giant bonfire, sending sparks up into the cold air.

"It's too late!" Mama cried. "Get back, everyone! Get back! Don't get hurt!"

As they backed away, the cabin roof crashed down into the flames with a roar. All they could do was watch as what was left of their home went up in black smoke.

Aunt Inger hugged Mama, and Mama hugged Kirsten and Peter, and Anna and Lisbeth hugged each other.

Tears rolled down Mama's face. "We're all safe, that's the most important thing," she said softly. She pressed Peter and Kirsten against her. "You two are safe. The baby is safe. Kirsten even saved our trunk. But what will we ever do now?"

"You'll come live in our house with us!" Aunt Inger said. "It won't be so bad, you'll see. You can start over again. Don't cry, dears!"

But Kirsten couldn't stop crying. Their pillows were burning, and their blankets, and their sweaters, and even the diapers for Britta. Their spoons were burning, and their tin plates and mugs, and even the washtub and the mixing bowls. All they had left in the world were the clothes on their backs and the things in the trunk.

How could they possibly get along? How could they possibly start over? And what would Papa say when he heard that their home had burned to the ground? She buried her face in Mama's shawl and wept.

# GOOD NEWS?

"I like it *better* with everyone living here! It's cozy!" Anna said. She was setting out bowls for the potato soup Aunt Inger had made. "And it's much warmer with four of us in our bed, isn't it, Lisbeth?"

Lisbeth cut thick slices of bread to go with the soup. "It's warmer with Kirsten and Peter in our bed, but Peter kicks," she said.

"I do not kick!" Peter said. "Anyway, you talk in your sleep, Lisbeth! Last night you sat straight up and pulled the blankets off, and you didn't even know it! I wish I could sleep in a drawer, like Britta."

"I wish you'd sleep on the floor, like Lars!" Lisbeth said.

"Stop it, children!" Aunt Inger said. "Don't fuss about what can't be helped. Here, come have some soup."

"Is there enough soup for John and Mary, too?" Lars said. "They're coming soon. John and I are going to set beaver traps today." Lars was rubbing musk oil on the traps to hide the smell of his hands. Animals wouldn't come near a trap that smelled of humans.

"Yes, there's enough soup to share with them," Aunt Inger said. "Thank goodness the vegetables in your root cellar didn't burn."

"I hope they bring some bowls!" Lisbeth said. "We only have enough bowls for the eight of us."

"They can have their soup from a cup. No one goes hungry in our home," Aunt Inger said. "Lisbeth, why are you in a bad mood today?"

"I can't help it," Lisbeth said. She rubbed her forehead as though a tight band pressed there. "I try to be cheerful, but I just can't be!"

Kirsten gave Lisbeth's shoulder a friendly nudge. It was very, very hard on everyone to be crammed together all day and all night. "I'm going to set traps with Lars and John," Kirsten said.

"So you'll have extra space at the table to play with your paper dolls."

Lisbeth tried to smile. "Thank you, Kirsten."

With a bang! bang! bang! some-one knocked at the cabin door. Peter unlatched it and John burst in. His sister Mary was right on his heels. Their cheeks were red and their brown eyes glowed. Kirsten thought she'd never seen such big, happy smiles as theirs.

"Hello! We've got soup for you two," Lars said.

"And we've got news for you!" John said. He stamped snow off his boots and pulled off his mittens.

"What news do you have for us?" Mama said quickly. She bounced the baby on her knee to keep her quiet.

Mary pulled folded papers from her pocket. "Some mail came to Mr. Berkhoff's store! He sent it to our house because we're closer to town than you are. We got a letter from our father, and here are two letters for the Larsons!"

Aunt Inger put the soup ladle right back in the

pot and took the letter Mary handed her. Mama gave the baby to Kirsten and took the other letter. Everyone, even John and Mary, crowded around the table to hear the news.

Aunt Inger's lips moved as she read the letter from Uncle Olav. "He's well," she said. "He's making good money. He misses us, of course!" She smiled at Lisbeth and Anna. "He says when the thaw comes in April, they'll float the logs downstream to the sawmills. Then he'll be heading home."

Mama spread her letter on the table and bent over it. After she'd read a few lines to herself she started reading out loud:

"The logging is going well. I hope to make a hundred dollars this winter. With that money and the money from your pelts, we can buy more land to farm."

"A hundred dollars! That *is* good news!" Lars cried.

But Mama's eyes filled with tears. She covered Papa's letter with her hands. "Papa hasn't gotten *my* letter yet. He doesn't know our cabin burned down. Building another cabin will take every bit of the money he'll earn. There won't be enough for land of our own."

Anna's eyes filled with tears, too. When anyone cried, she always cried with them. "But we'll help you build a cabin!"

"I know you'll help us build," Mama said. She squeezed Anna's hand. "But starting over is so hard! When we came to America, we hoped to have a good house like the one we left behind in Sweden. Now we don't even have beds of our own."

Aunt Inger tossed her head as though shaking off all their troubles. "John, you said your family had good news. Tell us your good news!"

"Yes, tell them!" Mary said. She squeezed onto the bench beside Kirsten.

John jumped up off the trunk where he'd been sitting. "Listen to this! Father writes that he's going to be the manager of a logging camp! He'll run the whole camp. He'll be in charge of all the other men. And here's the best part—it's an Oregon camp!"

"Ore-gon camp?" Peter said. "What's Ore-gon?"

"*Where* is Oregon," Lisbeth corrected him.

*"Starting over is so hard!" Mama said.*
*"Now we don't even have beds of our own."*

"Oregon is a place."

"Oregon's a place far, far west, beyond the prairie and even the mountains." John was so excited that he slapped his leg as he spoke. "There are big forests of redwood and spruce to cut in Oregon. It's fine logging country!"

"How will your father travel all that way west to Oregon?" Mama asked.

"In a covered wagon on the Oregon Trail," John said. "But it's not just Father who's going to Oregon! Our whole family will go west! We'll sell our house, and with the money we'll buy a wagon and oxen and every- thing we need. In the spring, when Father comes home, we'll join a wagon train and head west for Oregon!"

"The Oregon Trail!" Lars almost shouted. "I'd give anything to be going with you!"

Kirsten wanted to be happy for John and Mary and their family. But her spirits sank low. Mary was one of her closest friends. John was almost like another brother. When they left for Oregon, she would miss them very, very much.

"Everything's always changing," Kirsten said softly.

"I like things to change," Lars said. "I like things to be new!"

"Me, too!" John said. "And everything's new in Oregon!"

Everyone started talking at the same time. "We'll miss you!" "When will you leave?" "Are there schools in Oregon?" "Are there stores?"

Kirsten thought that everyone was excited and happy except her. She was half-happy and half-sad.

She slipped her arm around Mary's waist. "Mary, when you leave for Oregon, we might never see you again," Kirsten said. That was the sad part.

"We can write letters to each other," Mary said.

"Anyway, *I'll* see you again!" Lars said confidently. "I'll come out to Oregon as soon as I can!"

"We'll meet out there," John said. "Maybe we can lead wagon trains together, Lars!"

Then Aunt Inger clanked the soup ladle against the pot to get attention. "The Stewarts' move to Oregon is good for them and good for you, too," she said to Mama. "The Stewarts want to sell their house. Your house has burned, and you need a new one. You can buy the Stewarts' house. Then they'll have the money they need to move west, and you'll have the home you want. Isn't that wonderful?"

Mama folded Papa's letter and slipped it into her apron pocket. "It would be wonderful to buy the Stewarts' house if we had the money for it."

"How much will your house cost, John?" Aunt Inger said. She spread her hands on her hips the way she did when she bargained with Mr. Berkhoff at his store.

"Father told us to sell the house and furniture for five hundred dollars," John said.

Aunt Inger pursed her lips and frowned. Now she didn't look so happy. "Five hundred dollars for your house and furniture? Your house has four rooms and each one has a window. It has a good wooden floor and a shingle roof. Five hundred dollars is a fair price, all right. But it *is* a lot of money."

"Papa wrote he'll only make a hundred dollars cutting logs," Mama said softly.

"But don't forget we're going to sell the pelts from our trap line," Lars said. "Then maybe we'll have enough money to buy the house."

"Even if you caught something in every trap every day, we still wouldn't have five hundred dollars," Mama said. "It's better not to hope to buy a house like the Stewarts'. It's better just to plan to build another little cabin like the one we had. That's all we can do." She sighed and took the baby back from Kirsten.

Aunt Inger sighed, too. "Come on, children, eat this good soup while it's hot. And you two, thank you for bringing us the letters. Let's hear some more about this place called Oregon."

# OLD JACK

"We could set these new beaver traps downstream," Kirsten said as she and Lars set out toward the stream a few days later. "I've seen beaver dams there. Near their dams is a good place to trap them."

"Good idea," Lars said. He pulled a big toboggan piled with the traps he'd prepared. "I say we give it a try."

"I say we do, too," Kirsten said. Her hands and feet tingled in the cold afternoon, but she wanted to be as hopeful and determined as Lars.

Today, John was checking the old trap line by himself so Lars and Kirsten could set traps for a new one. They were working extra hard because soon spring would come and the trapping season would be over. The Stewarts needed money for their move to Oregon. The Larsons needed a lot of money for a new home. So the children needed all the furs they could possibly trap, and there was no time to waste!

As Kirsten and Lars walked along the stream, Kirsten looked for trails of bubbles frozen in the ice. Beavers made the bubbles when they swam under the ice from their nests to shore. Each time Kirsten found a bubble trail, Lars dug a hole in the ice and lowered a trap into the water. The next time a beaver came this way, it would swim into their trap.

But there weren't as many bubble trails along this part of the stream as they'd hoped. When dusk came, they still had several traps left to set.

"We'll have to take these traps home with us," Lars said. "We can't stay out any longer. It will be dark soon."

"But look, Lars, here's a great spot!" Kirsten said. Right at her feet a trail of bubbles came to the bank. "Let's set just one more trap before we go back!"

Lars chopped a hole in the ice with his pick. Kirsten lowered the trap through the hole and into the water. As they turned back to their toboggan, an owl swooped low over their heads.

Lars peered after the owl and frowned. "Kirsten, if the owls are out, it's even later than I thought. We've got to hurry home."

The owl's hoot made Kirsten tremble. She'd heard stories about settlers who were caught in the woods at night. In this cold, she and Lars could freeze to death. Or a wolf might get them. "Let's run, Lars!" she said.

"It's hard to run in snowshoes," Lars said.

"Maybe we could take a shortcut through the woods," Kirsten said. "That would be faster than following the stream. I think that if we follow the North Star, we'll find the farm. Come on, let's go!"

In a short time they were away from the stream and into the deep woods. Lars kept his eye on the North Star and led the way. But there was no trail to follow, and it was hard to pull the toboggan.

"It's going to be dark soon. I wish we had a lantern!" Kirsten said. Then she spotted snowshoe tracks in the snow. "Lars, look!" she cried.

"Someone's made a trail here!"

Lars crouched down to study
the tracks. "These look like they
were made with old-fashioned
snowshoes. I bet they're Old

Jack's! John told me that Old Jack lived somewhere
in this part of the woods. If this is Old Jack's trail,
we're in luck!"

"Why?" Kirsten asked.

"Because we can follow the trail to where he
lives, that's why," Lars said. "He'll lend us a lantern,
I'm sure of it."

"Old Jack sounds spooky to me," Kirsten said.
"I'm scared of him."

"Are you more scared of Old Jack or of losing
our way in the woods?" Lars said.

Again the owl hooted, and now there were faint
howls that might be coyotes. Or wolves. Kirsten
hugged herself. "I'm more scared of losing our way,"
she said in a very small voice.

"Then let's follow these tracks and see if we can
find Old Jack's," Lars said. He took the lead as they
turned onto the snowshoe trail.

The trail led them into a ravine. As they followed

the trail, the ravine got more and more narrow. Rocky bluffs rose on both sides, like walls. There was no room for a cabin here.

Then Kirsten spotted a rough plank set into the rocks. It almost looked like a door. Firewood was stacked by it. She pointed. "Look," she said. "There's a door. There must be a cave behind it. Someone has made a home in a cave."

"This has got to be Old Jack's!" Lars said.

"But Old Jack's not here," Kirsten said. "Look, there's no smoke coming out of his chimney."

"Even if he's not here, we can borrow a lantern," Lars said.

If Old Jack wasn't in the cave she didn't have to be scared, Kirsten thought. She followed Lars.

Drifted snow piled against the door. It didn't look like anyone had been through that door for several days. Lars knocked. No one answered. He rattled the latch.

"The door's unlatched," Lars said. He shoved at the boards with both hands, but the door didn't give. "Come on, Kirsten, help me get this door open."

338

Kirsten ducked under Lars's arms and put her shoulder against the planks.

"One, two, three, push!" Lars said. They both shoved as hard as they could. The door creaked and then suddenly swung in. Kirsten was pushing so hard she fell onto her knees inside the cave. Lars tumbled in against her.

For a moment she couldn't see anything at all. And then, right there in front of her, she made out a man sitting against the rocky wall! He was dressed in leather. And he was looking right at them!

At first Kirsten couldn't get her breath. Then she screamed. She scrambled to her feet and started to run. Lars grabbed her shoulders.

"Kirsten! Don't run! He won't hurt us."

"He *will* hurt us!" Kirsten cried.

Lars shook her to make her be still. "Kirsten! He *can't* hurt us. He couldn't hurt anyone, even if he wanted to. Old Jack's dead."

Kirsten peeked around Lars at the man sitting stiffly on the floor. His face was white. There was no cloud of breath at his lips. His eyes were glazed over. Lars was right—the man was dead.

"Oh, Lars! What will we do now?" Kirsten whispered.

Lars took a deep breath. "We'll find his flint and light a lantern. Then we'll think what to do."

Lars found the lantern, and Kirsten found the flint stone by the fire hole. She struck the flint stone until sparks set fire to a bit of hay. Then Lars lit the wick of the lantern. In the flickering light they could see Old Jack better. He was an old man with a white beard and rough hands. His pants and jacket were deerskin. He made Kirsten think of an animal of the forest—a fox, maybe.

"Poor Old Jack!" she said.

Lars pulled Old Jack's fur cap down over the dead man's eyes. "Rest in peace, Old Jack," he said.

"Rest in peace," Kirsten repeated after Lars.

"How do you think Old Jack could have died?" Kirsten asked.

"He was an old, old man," Lars said slowly. "He probably sat down to rest and his heart stopped beating. After a while the fire burned out, and his body froze."

Kirsten couldn't stop trembling. "Let's take the lantern and go home. Let's get away from here!"

"We're much, much safer in this cave than we are in the woods," Lars said. "Let's look around."

Kirsten was frightened, but Lars seemed sure of himself. She stayed by his side as he found a tin cup, an iron pot, a skinning knife, a few stretcher boards with mink and marten pelts on them. Then Lars lifted the lantern high so they could see into the back of the cave.

At first all Kirsten saw were some Indian blankets on a pile of straw. Then she made out a stack of furs piled all the way up to the roof of the cave.

Lars drew in a sharp breath. "Look at that, Kirsten! Look at all those pelts! Old Jack's trapped twice as many pelts as we have, and all of them the finest fur!" He stroked one of the mink pelts. "He was the best trapper around here, that's for sure. There aren't any more like him!"

Kirsten looked down at Old Jack's body. "John said Old Jack doesn't have any family at all."

"No, he was alone in the world," Lars said.

"What will happen to Old Jack's body?" Kirsten

*"Look at that, Kirsten!" Lars said.*
*"Look at all those pelts! And all of them the finest fur!"*

said. "I wish Papa were here to tell us what to do!"

"Papa always knows what's right," Lars said. He took off his woolen cap and scratched his head, then he bit his lower lip. "Kirsten, do you know what I think Papa would tell us?"

"What, Lars?"

"He'd say that we have to bury Old Jack, that's what," Lars said.

"But we *can't* bury Old Jack," Kirsten said. "We can't dig him a grave while the ground is frozen."

"Then we'll have to come back and bury him in the spring," Lars said. "Papa would never leave a body unburied, I know that." He paced back and forth as he thought. "Do you know what else Papa would tell us?"

Kirsten shook her head.

"Papa would say that if Old Jack doesn't have kin, then his things belong to whoever finds them. And we found them."

Kirsten plopped down on the little three-legged stool by the fire hole. "Do you mean they're ours like finders-keepers?"

"No, it's not like finders-keepers. If Old Jack were alive and we found something he'd lost, we would give it back to him. But he's dead and gone, so we can't give him back these furs. We can't give him anything but a proper burial. He doesn't even have a family to do that."

Kirsten looked again at Old Jack, then at the big stack of furs. "Are you sure Papa would say Old Jack's things are ours?" she asked.

"I'm sure!" Lars said.

"Even all his furs?" Kirsten asked again.

"Even his furs," Lars said firmly.

"Oh, Lars," Kirsten breathed. "Those furs are worth a lot of money!"

"That's what I'm thinking, Kirsten. And I'm thinking how much we need money now. Old Jack's furs might even be worth enough to buy the Stewarts' house."

Kirsten rested her chin on her hands. She wanted to be glad about the furs, but she felt tears brim at her eyes. "Lars, it's a dark night with no moon. Even with a lantern, I don't know if we can find our way home. And it's bitter cold! How will we ever take so many furs with us?"

Lars was piling up kindling and split wood. He

lit the fire and knelt beside her. "Don't cry, Kirsten. I have a plan. Just listen to me."

Kirsten scrubbed at her cheeks. Lars could always make a plan, she thought. If she had to be lost in the woods, she was glad she was with her big brother!

"First," Lars said, "it's much too dangerous to try to get home in the dark. Second, we're safe here from the cold and from wolves. So we have to stay until it's light. Third, in the morning we'll load the pelts onto our toboggan and follow the stream home."

Still Kirsten was troubled. "But what about Old Jack? We have to bury him! Especially if we're going to take his furs."

"Of course we'll do right by Old Jack," Lars said. "For now we'll cover him with a blanket. In the morning, before we leave, we'll pile stones against his door so animals can't get in. When Papa comes back in the spring, the ground will be thawed. Papa and I will dig Old Jack a grave. We'll bury him, and Papa will say the burying prayers."

Kirsten rocked back and forth on the little stool. "Lars, it's a good plan. But I don't want to stay the whole night in this cave with a dead man!"

When Lars folded his arms he looked just like Papa delivering a lecture. "Old Jack was a good man and his soul is in heaven. There's nothing to be scared of."

He set a thick log on the fire. "Now we've got to get some rest. I'll keep watch, and you lie down on that blanket and sleep."

Kirsten shivered, but she did as Lars said. She lay down on the blanket and drew her knees up under her chin. She closed her eyes tightly and tried to sleep. But she was as wide awake as if morning had come already.

"Lars?" she whispered.

"Are you thinking about Old Jack?" Lars said.

"I'm thinking how scared Mama will be when we don't come home tonight," Kirsten said.

"Mama knows we can find shelter," Lars said. "Remember, once you and Papa hid in a cave during a snowstorm. Go to sleep now."

Kirsten didn't think she would sleep. How *could* she? But when she opened her eyes, a line of morning light showed around the door. An Indian blanket covered Old Jack's body. Potatoes roasted in the coals of the fire. And Lars was already tying the furs into bundles to load onto the toboggan.

"Get yourself up!" Lars cried. "We've got to take these furs home to Mama!"

# WELCOME HOME

Soon March rains began to melt the deep snow. When the ice on the streams thawed, the trapping season was over. But with Old Jack's pelts and the ones from the trap line, the Larsons had enough money to buy the Stewarts' house. Papa wrote that he and Mr. Stewart had shaken hands on the deal. "Make our new house ready," the letter said. "I'll be home in April!"

Mr. Stewart was the first one to come back from the logging camp. Soon after he arrived, the Stewarts loaded up their things and set off to join the wagon train for Oregon. The next day, the Larsons got ready to move into their new house.

Everyone helped. Anna folded clean diapers on the bed where Britta played with her rattle. Lisbeth and Kirsten packed sweaters and shawls into the blue trunk. Lars carried out the traps, and Peter stacked wood for the stove into the wagon. Aunt Inger and Mama packed flour and salt and coffee and other things for cooking into a wooden box.

"Here's an extra skillet," Aunt Inger said. "Take it along. And here's a stew pot I don't often use."

"You've given us so much already," Mama said. "You mustn't give us your pots and pans, too."

But Aunt Inger put the pot into the box. "How will you feed the children without a pan to cook in? Did the Stewarts leave any plates behind?"

"They said they would leave some plates and spoons and cups," Mama said. "They even left some of their furniture, and straw mattresses and a few blankets, too. A covered wagon doesn't hold very much."

Aunt Inger put her fists into her waist and smiled at the small pile of the Larsons' belongings. "You could put everything here into a covered wagon and still have lots of room left over!"

Mama sank down at the table and sighed. "If the Stewarts hadn't left behind their table, Papa would have to build one for us before we could have supper."

"Where is Papa?" Kirsten said. "Mr. Stewart came home more than a week ago. He said Papa and Uncle Olav would come on the next boat."

"Papa will be here as soon as he can," Mama said. "I want to have our new house clean and shining for him. I want him to walk in and find us all just as he left us last winter."

"He'll find that Britta's grown twice as big!" Aunt Inger said. She gave the baby a kiss on top of her blond head, and then another kiss to Anna.

Anna made a little moan like the sound of wind under the door. "Ohhh! It will be so lonely without all of you sharing the farm with us!" she said.

Kirsten felt lonely, too, the way she'd felt when she waved good-bye to Mary and John and their family. She sat down on the bed beside Anna and took her hand. "We're going to live just a few miles away, Anna. We'll see each other often."

Anna put her head on Kirsten's shoulder. "I'll

miss talking at bedtime. Can I sleep at your house someday?"

"Of course you can," Kirsten said. "I'll be alone in the trundle bed until Britta outgrows her cradle."

Mama put her hands on Kirsten's and Anna's knees. "There's no reason for those long faces, girls. Today we're moving into our new house, and before long Papa will be with us again."

But Kirsten saw that Mama blinked tears, too. Happy times could bring tears just like sad times.

Aunt Inger pulled a soft old carpetbag from under the bed and scooped the clean diapers into it. "We won't put this carpetbag into the trunk. You'll need these diapers before you need anything else. Now let's get your things into the wagon," Aunt Inger said. "Lisbeth and Anna and I will come along later with a big pot of soup for your first supper in your new home!"

♥

Kirsten had run up the lane to the Stewarts' house many, many times. But today, as Lars drove their wagon up the lane, the house looked new and

special and full of surprises, like a gift. *This is our house,* Kirsten whispered to herself. Every night from now on her family would sleep under that wide shingled roof. Every morning they would walk out that door onto their very own land.

Peter jumped out of the wagon even before Lars reined in the horse. Caro bounded out right at Peter's heels and scampered to the door, barking as if he knew he belonged here now. Britta smiled and bounced in Mama's lap as though she'd like to run, too. Kirsten tied Blackie to the hitching post, and Mama climbed down out of the wagon.

"Open the door, Kirsten," Mama said. "Peter, you carry Britta so she doesn't get in the way and get hurt. We'll take the trunk inside first."

Kirsten opened the front door and peered inside. She had been in this house so often she knew it almost as well as Aunt Inger's house. But without John and Mary here, the house seemed quiet and empty. "Hello?" Kirsten called, and the echo greeted her, "Hello!"

The door opened into the big kitchen. Peter carried Britta inside. Then Lars dragged the trunk

*"I didn't realize how heavy this trunk is!" Mama said.*
*"How did you manage to pull it out of the fire all by yourself, Kirsten?"*

into the doorway, and Mama and Kirsten came behind to push it over the sill.

"I didn't realize how heavy this trunk is!" Mama said. "How did you manage to pull it out of the fire all by yourself, Kirsten?"

"I was so frightened I was strong," Kirsten said.

"And there weren't so many things packed in the trunk then," Peter said. "I bet I could have saved the trunk, too!"

"You saved the baby, Peter!" Kirsten said.

"This trunk came all the way from Sweden," Lars said. "Now it's got to come just a little farther. Push one more time!"

He yanked and they shoved. The trunk scraped through the door, and suddenly Kirsten and Mama were inside the house, too.

 Sunlight shone through the glass window as though a hundred candles lit the room. The house smelled of the bread Mrs. Stewart had baked for her family's journey to Oregon, and of lye soap. Peter set Britta down on the scrubbed floor. She crawled to the table and pulled herself up and laughed, as though she announced, "Here we are!"

Mama spread her arms wide and gazed around the kitchen as though she saw it for the very first time. "Look how big it is!" she said. "And we have a fine cookstove, and cup-boards for our dishes! And a chest for our clothes! And shelves, too, lots of them!"

"We have a wood floor like the one at Aunt Inger's!" Lars said.

"And we have a good strong table," Mama said, "and even chairs!" Mama stroked the back of one. "When we sit at our table, we can look out the window and see that big maple tree." She sighed. "Oh, this is a real home, isn't it! This is the home your papa and I dreamed we'd have in America."

Peter dashed into the next room. "We have two big beds and a trundle bed, too!"

Kirsten followed Peter. There was another glass window in this room. She had spent many happy hours with Mary on the bench under the window. Here they'd practiced their reading and made up stories. Here they'd played with their paper dolls and told secrets and made promises. Kirsten knelt on the bench. This would be a good place for her

and Lisbeth and Anna to work on their quilting, she thought.

Kirsten put her fingertips on the cool window-pane. She could see the rope swing in the maple tree. She and Peter would love that swing! When Britta was older, they'd swing her in it, too. And under the maple was a nice patch of shade where Mama could do her mending on hot summer days. It would be good to live in this house.

A bit of paper tucked into the corner of the window frame caught her eye. She pulled the paper free and unfolded it.

The note was in Mary's pretty handwriting.

*Dear Kirsten,*
*Please be happy in your new house! The*
*next time I write it will be from*
*Oregon! Don't forget your loving friends,*
*Mary and John*
*P.S. John made the little*
*toy for you!*

Kirsten looked carefully at the little toy. On one side was a picture of a bird cage. On the other side, a bluebird. When Kirsten spun the toy, the bird seemed to fly into the cage. There it was, safe and happy, like Kirsten in her new home. The secret good-bye from Mary and John made her heart even lighter, like a bird fluttering under her ribs. She put the letter and the toy into her pocket. Her friends wouldn't forget her, and she would never forget them, not ever!

Then a figure came into view far down the road. Kirsten pressed her forehead against the window-pane to see better. A man was walking in long strides. Could it be Papa? Yes, it was Papa! He was back from the logging camp at last. And he was just in time to be with them in their new house!

"Mama!" Kirsten called. "Papa's back! Here he comes right now!" She ran into the kitchen and opened the door.

Peter skidded out through the door with Lars right behind him. Mama hurried with the baby hugged to her shoulder. "Welcome home! Welcome home, Papa!" Kirsten called as they all hurried to the gate to meet him.

LOOKING BACK 1854

# A Peek Into the Past

<br>

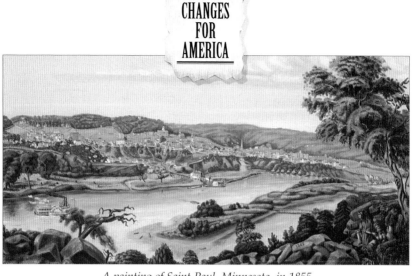

**CHANGES FOR AMERICA**

*A painting of Saint Paul, Minnesota, in 1855*

As Kirsten grew up, more and more people traveled west across America to start new farms. New settlers moved closer to one another, and farm villages turned into bustling little towns with churches, schools, and town halls. There were more stores because there were more farmers with more things to buy and sell. Families started to plan weekly trips to town, not only to shop but

*Farm families liked to get together for dances and dinners.*

also to visit with friends. They held socials and dances and church suppers so that neighbors could meet. The lonely times of the Larson family's first years on the frontier were over.

360

Farms weren't isolated from the rest of America, either. The railroad, that "iron horse" that carried Kirsten and her family to the edge of the frontier, was linking cities and farms across the country. By the time Kirsten was twenty-four years old, the first *transcontinental railroad* in the world joined America from coast to coast.

Because of railroads, farm families didn't have to make everything they needed the way pioneers did. They could buy things directly from stores in faraway cities. Farmers would study a store's newspaper ads, then mail an order and money to the store. Trains delivered the mail, and the store sent

*Pioneers bought many things they needed out of catalogues.*

out the things the farmer had ordered on the next train. By the time Kirsten was a young woman, this kind of shopping started a new industry—the mail-order

*Trains carried the mail across America. Railroads also carried the things people ordered from catalogues.*

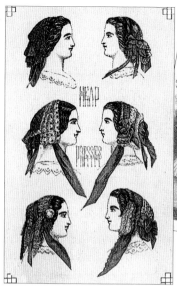

*Godey's Lady's Book showed American women the latest fashions.*

business. Today, people still shop from mail-order catalogues, except now they place orders on the telephone or the Internet, and their orders are shipped by trucks and airplanes as well as trains. Of course, there were no trucks or airplanes when Kirsten was growing up.

Trains also carried ideas to America's farms. Farm girls and women read about the latest fashions in magazines that came to them by train. And families waited eagerly for the train to bring the next part, or *installment,* of the popular stories that were published in monthly magazines. There weren't radios or televisions for news and entertainment back then.

Trains also brought new farm equipment. As Kirsten grew up, factories were making

*Big machines made men's farm work easier.*

*Farm families could sell extra crops.*

stronger plows and machines like threshers and reapers. These machines helped farmers produce much more food than their families could ever eat. So farmers sent their extra crops back to towns and cities where the food could be processed and sold. Farms like the one Kirsten lived on became "the nation's breadbasket," feeding people throughout America.

Farms also got bigger and bigger, until they were too big for a family to work alone. When Kirsten married, she and her family would not have worked together in the fields the way the Larson family did. Instead, Kirsten's children would go to school and her husband would work the land with the help of *hired hands,* or farm helpers.

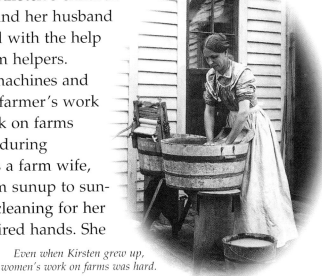

Although new machines and hired hands made a farmer's work easier, women's work on farms didn't change much during Kirsten's lifetime. As a farm wife, she would work from sunup to sundown, cooking and cleaning for her big family and the hired hands. She

*Even when Kirsten grew up, women's work on farms was hard.*

363

*A modern kitchen like this still didn't have running water.*

would milk cows, take care of the chickens, sell eggs, churn butter, and tend a large garden so there would be plenty of food to preserve for winter.

Some modern equipment made Kirsten's life easier than Mama's had been. Kirsten probably cooked on a brand new cast-iron range that had an oven in it. But she still had to lug wood into the house to keep the stove full, a job that was just as heavy and hard for her as it had been for Mama. Kirsten probably had a pump outside in the yard so she wouldn't have to carry water

THE ✦ PATENT ✦ CLOTHES ✦ DRYER.

from the stream. But doing the laundry was still an all-day chore. She would pump water into a bucket, heat it on the stove, scrub the soiled clothes against a metal board in a washtub, hang them out to dry on a clothesline, then press them with a heavy iron she heated on the stove. In the evenings, Kirsten would mend and sew clothes for

*Heavy "sad irons" had to be heated on the stove.*

her large family, but a modern sewing machine made this chore easier than it had been for Mama. If she were lucky, Kirsten would get a pump in her kitchen by the time she was forty years old. But she would never have had electricity, running water, or an indoor toilet in her farm home.

*Kirsten's sewing machine was powered by her feet, not electricity.*

Although work on the farm continued to be hard, most American families chose to live on farms throughout the 1800s. People liked life on the farm because they enjoyed working together as families on land that had belonged to their parents. After all, a chance to own land of their own was the main reason that families like the Larsons had come to America in the first place, and people like Kirsten and her children were proud to keep that tradition alive.

## Meet the Author

Each night when JANET SHAW was a girl, she took out a flashlight and book hidden under her pillow and read until she fell asleep. She and her brother liked to act out stories, especially ones about sword fights and wild horses. Today, Ms. Shaw has three grown children. When they were small, she often pulled them in a big red wagon to the library, where they filled the wagon with so many books they had to walk back home. Janet Shaw lives in North Carolina with her husband and their two dogs, who sleep by her feet when she's writing.

♥

## Meet the Illustrator

RENÉE GRAEF works at her home in Milwaukee, Wisconsin, near Lake Michigan. She enjoys wearing hats and has a collection of over 150 hats hanging on her walls. Ms. Graef wears out three electric pencil sharpeners a year on the colored pencils she uses in her artwork.

# MORE TO DISCOVER!

While books are the heart of The American Girls Collection®, they are only the beginning. The stories in the Collection come to life when you act them out with the beautiful American Girls dolls and their exquisite clothes and accessories. To request a catalogue full of things girls love, you can send in this postcard, call **1-800-845-0005,** or visit our Web site at **americangirl.com**.

*Please send me an American Girl® catalogue.*

My name is _____

My address is _____

City _____ State _____ Zip _____
1961i

My birth date is _____/_____/_____ E-mail address _____
month   day   year

Parent's signature _____

## And send a catalogue to my friend:

My friend's name is _____

Address _____

City _____ State _____ Zip _____
1225i

If the postcard has already been removed from this book and you would like to receive an American Girl® catalogue, please send your name and address to:

*American Girl*
*P.O. Box 620497*
*Middleton, WI 53562-0497*

You may also call our toll-free number, **1-800-845-0005,** or visit our Web site at **americangirl.com**.

‖ ‖

Place
Stamp
Here

PO BOX 620497
MIDDLETON WI 53562-0497

|ı.|ı...||ı.|ı.||ıı.ı|ı|||ı.ı|ıı||ı|ı.|ıı.||ı|ı.|ıı.|ıı||ı|